THE TROUBLE WITH THE LAW

Billy Hall

Billy Hall, *The Trouble With The Law*

Published by Deo Volente Publishing
1614 Thunderbird
Las Cruces, NM 88011
Printed in the United States of America

ISBN: 978-0-9753446-6-8

CHAPTER

"How many bodies?"

"None."

A chill wind of premonition brushed the back of Levi's neck. "None? How can there be none?"

The District Superintendent of the Pinkerton Detective Agency smiled tightly. "That's what you're supposed to find out. You're paid to be a detective, remember?"

Levi ignored the bait. "How many wagons?"

"There were thought to be eighteen when they left Omaha. The last place they were seen was Bridger's Crossing. The charred remains of only seventeen wagons were counted, however."

"They were found just north of Elkhorn Crick?"

"They were found just north of Elkhorn Creek," the official corrected, emphasizing the pronunciation of 'creek.'

Levi pretended not to notice. "But they crossed the Platte at Bridger's."

"I believe I said that, yes."

"That's north of where they were found."

"Is that of some significance?"

"Might be. They followed the Platte up out of Nebraska, but stayed on the north side, instead of crossing over to the Oregon Trail on the south. Then they crossed the river at Bridger's. That means they changed direction. They either found what they were looking for, knew where they were going, got lost, or ran into something unexpected."

The supervisor folded his hands across his ample stomach and leaned back in his chair. He put his feet up on his desk. "They most certainly did find something they were not expecting. The Grim Reaper. They were massacred. Their entire wagon train was destroyed."

"Tell me about where they found it. What's the country like?"

"It was a place with little shelter and no water. Not a good camp site at all. It was along the bottom of a wide shallow draw, not too far off the stage road. It is uncertain why they were there and, especially, why they were not on the road itself. The stage coach driver spotted multiple wisps of smoke as he passed on the weekly stage run. He made no effort to investigate, of course, because he had the responsibility of the stage coach. He reported it, however, when he changed teams. A cowboy, who chanced to be at the Horseshoe Stage Station, rode back to check it out. He is the one who found it. It had already been there for two or three days, he thought."

"Indians?"

"So he said."

"Indians leave the bodies lay. They may scalp 'em, but they leave the bodies where they fall."

William Snodgrass snorted, heaving his feet off his desk. "Indians are savages. They do as they please, with neither rhyme nor reason, without the sort of rational behavior that characterizes civilized, Christian people."

Levi shook his head. "They never please to carry off dead bodies, except their own folks. They might carry off some strong woman to work, or a pretty one for fun, or for an extra squaw. They might carry off some kids, to raise and keep. They like kids. They wouldn't carry off everyone."

Snodgrass's irritation was evident. "I am impressed to learn that you are our resident expert on Indian behavior now."

Levi's lips compressed to a thin line. "I lived with the Shoshoni some. I know Indians. If Indians killed those people, someone else came along and hauled them off and buried 'em."

The superintendent's frown deepened. "You would be well advised to save your conclusions until after you have investigated. Pinkerton detectives, you will need to learn, do not jump to conclusions."

Levi ignored the remark. "What about the army?"

"What about the army?"

"When a whole wagon train gets wiped out, it seems like the army ought to get involved."

"They were notified. They sent someone to investigate. The usual forms were filled out and forwarded to Washington. That, as usual, will be the end of the matter with the army."

"How did Pinkerton get involved?"

Snodgrass flushed irritably. He did not enjoy having to share information or reasons with his subordinates. He sighed in resignation. "The Sicklemans are a wealthy and important family in Omaha, as well as other eastern cities. Their daughter married beneath her station and against their will. She married a man with romantic visions of journeying westward to fulfill his destiny on the great American frontier. He eschewed legitimacy and civilization in favor of adventure and independence. After spurning their very generous offer to establish him in the family business, he took his wife and infant son and joined a wagon train. That wagon train. The Sicklemans are determined to know what happened to their daughter, her husband and their grandson."

"They were told it was Indians?"

"They were. They are less than satisfied with that. They want to know what Indians, whether it was a tribal action or a small band of renegades, why they attacked that wagon train, and they want them brought to justice."

"And if it wasn't Indians?" Levi persisted.

"The army is convinced it was Indians. I am convinced it

was Indians. I think they are convinced it was Indians. I see no reason to challenge that premise."

"Do they know Indians don't carry off people they kill, don't bury 'em, and don't hide the bodies?"

Levi's questions were becoming a source of personal irritation. Both Snodgrass's face and voice conveyed that information eloquently as he replied. "They do not want a dissertation on the customs of the American savages. Nor do I. I just want you to get up there and find out what happened. If you find the particular group of Indians who perpetrated the violence, you are authorized to arrest them and bring them back here for hanging. If you are unable to arrest them, you are authorized to kill any or all of them, as necessary. If you need assistance in the dispatch of that task, you may hire as many men with guns as necessary to complete it. If you are unable to do so, you may send a telegram requesting reinforcements. We will send ten of our best men, at your disposal and under your command."

Levi whistled. "This Sickleman family must be paying some pretty big money to find their daughter. I was never offered any help before."

"That is none of your concern. Your concern is earning your own wages. You have been assigned only minor investigations prior to this date. You have fulfilled those assignments admirably. That is why you are now being given this greater responsibility. There is one other thing: I do want the savages' bodies sundered from their souls, if they have souls, in such a time and place as a photographer can be dispatched to make a tintype. The family will want to see the evidence of justice exacted."

"What if it ain't Indians?" Levi asked one more time.
He wasn't sure he doubted it was Indians at all. It just pro-

vided him too much pleasure to irritate his corpulent boss. Once again, he was most successful.

Snodgrass looked like Levi must have lost his sanity entirely. "Who else could it possibly be? Who else kills women and children? Who in the world would have a motive to wipe out an entire wagon train? Who else kills people with bows and arrows?"

Levi was not impressed with the argument. "I don't know any Indians that would have a reason to do it the way this was done, either."

"You exasperate me! Since when do Indians need a reason to kill white people?"

"I thought you didn't want a dissertation on the customs of the American savage."

The Pinkerton official's face deepened to purple. He sputtered as he answered. "You thought correctly. You will be well advised to curtail your insolence and get about your job. You are dismissed."

Levi sat without moving long enough to irritate, just a little more, the pompous pretender who controlled his life. He thought again about throwing in his chips, and finding a job as a regular lawman. He knew he would never be content with that, though. It would be the same situation. It would just be a different face across the desk.

To envision a life other than as a lawman was out of the question. The only way his gifts could be used without making a pariah of him was to work for the law. He had, too many times already, been called a freak because he was too fast, too strong, too accurate, too quick.

Accordingly, he had hired out to the Pinkerton Agency as a range detective. It had its advantages. It also had its drawbacks. Snodgrass was the prime example of the latter, at the moment.

That's the trouble with the law, he thought. *You always have to answer to some chair polisher who couldn't find his rear end with both hands out on the mountain.*

Finally he shrugged. He stood up slowly, skillfully timing his moves just an instant ahead of his superior's limit of patience. "I'll ride out that way tomorrow or the next day." He could almost hear the blood rush to Snodgrass's face. Without looking, he could see the veins once more standing out on that shiny, carefully perfumed forehead. Hiding a grin, he closed the door without waiting for a response.
As he stepped out of the shade into the hot dry air, he stopped. Cheyenne was becoming quite a city. The noise of the bustling street pounded at him. The dust raised by the incessant traffic filled his nostrils. The smell of too many horses in too little space clung to that dust.
"Anything will be better than being stuck here in town any longer," he said aloud to himself.

Glancing along the street, he saw a cowboy leaning against a store front watching him. The cowboy quickly ducked his head, dropping his hat brim across his face too quickly for Levi to get a good look at him. The man turned and ambled away along the rough board sidewalk, trying just a little too hard to seem casual.

Levi watched him out of sight, but the cowboy showed no more interest in him, nor did he turn around.
"I wonder if he was waitin' there to get a look at me comin' out of the Pinkerton office?" Levi asked himself. "If he was, I wonder why."

As he said it, that cold wind blew down his spine again. He shivered in spite of the oppressive heat. He sighed and headed for the hotel to pack his things. Whatever stood before him had just as well not be kept waiting.

CHAPTER

"I hate this blasted wind!" Levi said aloud to his horse.

The horse bobbed his head, shaking the reins in silent agreement. The wind had been blowing just as hard since he left Cheyenne. He hated the way it fought to lift his hat from his head. It made him pull it down uncomfortably tight and keep it there. He hated the way it scoured his skin until it felt raw, sucking the moisture from it, leaving it hard and scaly. He hated the sound of it, constantly rushing in his ears. He hated the way it kept pulling the end of his neckerchief loose and flapping it against his chin. He hated the way it masked all the other sounds of the country. He hated the way it ground away at him, grinding, grinding, as if trying to wear away his soul.

The wind completely hid the sound of the other's approach. He chanced to glance back and saw a cowboy loping toward him along the main road. He had a hand in the air as though he were hailing Levi. His mouth was open, but the ceaseless wind whipped away any words he might have been shouting. Levi reined in, slipping the thong off the hammer of the Colt .45 in his holster.

A huge tumbleweed suddenly blew across the road right in front of the approaching cowboy. His horse reacted immediately, shying violently to the side. The cowboy jerked his hand back from waving at Levi to grab leather, but his hand slapped the horse's ear on the way by. The horse shied again, then began to buck frantically.

For several seconds Levi thought the cowboy would ride him. He gave it a valiant effort, especially for starting off balance from the get-go. Then the horse made an abrupt change of direction in mid-jump. The sudden switch caused the rider to lose his right stirrup. Sensing the rider's sudden disadvantage, the horse redoubled the frenzy of his bucking. The cowboy fought vainly to regain the stirrup. As he succeeded, his boot slid all the way through the left stirrup. Off balance and helpless, he left the saddle. His right foot arched high above him as he fell, head downward.

As his head and shoulders struck the ground, the horse stopped bucking and began to run. The cowboy's boot remained through the left stirrup, securely anchoring his foot to the saddle of the runaway mount. If he made any sound, the wind tore it away before it reached Levi's ears.

Levi jammed the spurs to his horse's sides. The big buckskin gelding shot forward, reaching full stride in four jumps. Leaning forward, nearly against the horse's neck, Levi yelled, "Catch 'im, Buck!"

He shot past the rider, then his horse, staying on the right to avoid the cowboy bouncing and flopping along on the horse's left. He reached out and grabbed one flying rein as they passed, then began sawing on his own reins, pulling his own horse to a stop.
Even before they stopped, he knotted the runaway's rein to his own saddle horn and slid from the right side of his own animal. As his horse forced the other to come to a complete stop, Levi was already around the two horses, working to twist the stirrup so the unseated rider could pull his trapped foot free.

It came free with a jerk. Levi released the stirrup and stepped back. He knew his own horse would prevent the spooked mount from going any place until he settled down. He was far more concerned with the fate of the cowboy. The man lay still, jerking short gulps of air into his lungs.

"You all right?" he asked, as he bent over the gasping man.

"I've been better a time or two," the man on the ground gritted between gasps.

"He kick you some?"

The cowboy paused, sucking in great gulps of air. When he spoke, his voice was stronger. "Just in the head once or twice."

Levi began to relax. "I figured that, but I was wonderin' if he kicked anything that you use much."

There was no answer for a long minute. When the answer came, it ignored his dry attempt at humor altogether. "I hate that danged wind!"

Levi chuckled. "Me too. I wonder if it always blows like that around here?"

"Aw, no. No, it don't. About half the time it turns around and blows outa the other direction, just as hard."

"Well, that must mean you work around here somewhere. Can't say as I understand why, though. You could always leave. There's outfits you could ride for where the wind doesn't blow all the time."

The cowboy sat up amongst the sage brush and yucca. "I've tried. Honest, I've tried. I got clear over danged near to Utah once, then the wind came up an' blowed me right back again. Then I decided

I'd go along with it, instead o' fightin' it. I just went with it and let it blow me clear over into Nebraska. Trouble was, it blew this whole end o' Wyoming over there too. Then as soon as the wind stopped blowin', Wyoming just snapped right back here where it belonged, and there I was, right along with it."

"Sounds like a hard country to get out of."

"Oh, it's worse'n hard. It's impossible. Once you're here, you're just stuck. You'd just as well find a place to hire on, or else homestead. O' course, then you'll starve to death."

Levi kept his face as straight as the cowboys. "I sorta had it in mind to see some of the rest of the world."

"Me too," the cowboy agreed soberly, still sitting on the ground. "I will, too, now that I know how. You see, I started out tryin' to chase all over lookin' for it. I finally figured out I didn't have to. The way the wind blows around here, I just gotta latch onto a tree and wait. Sooner or later the rest of the world will just blow right past me. I can see it all without ever turnin' loose o' that tree. Most anytime now I 'spect to see Chinamen in them pigtails come blowin' past."

"I'll remember that the next time I get itchy feet. The trouble is, I ain't seen a tree in this end o' Wyoming to hang on to. Can you get to your feet okay?"

"I reckon. You see my hat?"

"Last I saw it, it was headin' for Nebraska without you. I was afraid you'd lost that one for good, till you told me about this wind. Now I ain't worried no more. It'll probably come back, right along with this end o' Wyoming, the first time the wind stops blowin'."

The cowboy struggled to his feet and walked around gingerly.

"Whatd'ya know! I don't think there's anything busted. I'm obliged. That danged ol' Roman-nosed sorrel woulda drug me to death if you hadn't a-been there. You musta caught 'im in less'n a dozen jumps."

"Buck's pretty fast," Levi agreed. "I saw your foot go through the stirrup, and knew you were in trouble before you hit the ground. Ol' Buck was already moving when you landed."

"Well, I sure am obliged," he said again. "I guess I'll ride a ways to see if I can find my hat."

"I got a pretty good idea where it left the road. I'll look with you." It took the pair of them nearly three hours to find the hat. It was lodged in a scrub cedar tree, about eight feet from the ground. The cowboy retrieved it, knocked the dirt and grass from it, reshaped it, and pulled it down firmly on his head. His mood changed immediately.

"There, now! That's better," he said. "My name's Wade. Wade Robinson. Most folks call me Doc."

"Doc?"

He grinned. "Just a handle. I kinda got a knack for nursin' sick cows, bringin' 'em around when they oughta die, getting breached calves out of 'em, that sorta thing."

"Good man to have around a place," Levi observed.
Wade shrugged modestly. "Makes it easy to hire on, most places, whenever I need a job."

The cowboy looked familiar, now that he had his hat on. The sense of having seen him somewhere niggled at the corners of Levi's mind, but he couldn't place where or when. Ignoring the feeling, he said, "Headin' somewhere in particular now?"

Wade hesitated. "Well, fact is I was sorta thinkin' about hirin' on to the W-W. I've worked there before and they treat their hands right. Fact is, I just been down to Cheyenne. Got my wages all blowed, so I'll probably head back to the W-W. Besides, it's back close to the mountains where this danged wind don't blow all the time."

"Where's the W-W?"

"You ain't heard of it? That wind blowed you in from quite a ways, didn't it?"

Levi opened his mouth, then shut it abruptly. That premonition tickled the hair on the back of his neck. Up to now he had thought to ride openly as a Pinkerton range detective. He had no idea why he was hesitant to disclose the fact to this open-faced cowboy whose life he had just saved. Nevertheless, the warning was there. He decided not to ignore it.

"My name's Wink Lee," he lied. "I hail from over toward Sweetwater. I'm just ridin' the grubline."

Wade folded his hands on his saddle horn and shifted his weight. "Well then, I'll tell you about this place, Wink Lee. The W-W brand belongs to Butch Westfal. It lays up in the edge of the mountains, maybe fifteen miles up La Bonte Crick from the stage station. He runs maybe three or four thousand head. They range up in the mountains in the summer, then on the flats along the crick in the winter. Great place. None better, as a matter of fact. You could do worse than hirin' on at the W-W. Why don't you ride along with me? We can both hire on together."

Levi pushed his hat up from his forehead. Instantly the wind whipped it from his head and sent it soaring away. Wade spurred his horse, stood tall in the stirrups, and caught it in mid-air. He wheeled his horse, slowing to a trot. The horse tossed his head, fighting for the freedom to run, as he pulled him to a stop instead.

Levi reached out and took the hat Wade extended to him. "Dang, I hate this wind," he said.

Wade laughed for the first time, an open, easy laugh that Levi liked. "You almost got it right. It ain't 'Dang, I hate this wind,' though. It's 'I hate this danged wind.' But you are already startin' to sound like me."

"I don't ride like you, though. I generally keep both feet in the stirrups," Levi shot back.

Wade assumed an affected look of wide-eyed innocence. "Well, that's fine when you're ridin', but how do you ever get off your horse when you're keepin' both feet in the stirrups?"

Levi mirrored his expression. "Well, when it's my idea to get off instead of my horse's idea, then I turn loose of the stirrups. Of course I most generally try to hit the ground with my feet first. My head's not hard enough to land on, like some fellers I've noticed lately."

"Yeah, but I figured if we're gonna ride together, one of us had oughta use his head."

"To land on, or to beat his horse's hooves with?"

"You mean that ain't what a head's supposed to be used for? If a fella had a really sharp mind, maybe he could even trim his horse's hooves while he was at it."

"Ain't what I use mine for."

"What do you use yours for?"

"To hold my hat, to keep it from blowin' away in this danged wind."

Wade shook his head. “You win,” he laughed.

They walked their horses back to the main road and turned north together. That night they camped in a sheltered spot along Cottonwood Creek. They chatted idly about the places they’d worked, and a few cowboys they learned they knew in common. Several times Levi started to reveal his role as a range detective. Each time that whisper of warning in his mind prevented him from doing so. He rolled into his blankets that night feeling an uneasiness he could not explain, and a foreboding he could not ignore.

CHAPTER

"What's left of the wagon train is just over them hills. You did hear about the wagon train, didn't you?"

Levi was instantly and fully alert. In spite of the bells ringing in his mind, he made an instant decision to feign ignorance. "What wagon train's that?"

Wade Robinson shoved his hat onto the back of his head and folded his hands on his saddle horn. It was uncommonly still. It was the first day since leaving Cheyenne without that grinding, wearing, persistent wind. Today was still, and it seemed wrong, somehow, as though nature were holding her breath.

"The burnt one," Wade responded without slowing his horse.

Levi decided to continue to play ignorant. "Burnt one? A wagon train burned?"

"It's right over that way," Wade nodded with his head toward the right side of the road.

"Really? How far?"

"Half a mile or so."

"You seen it?"

"Sure. I rode over to see it. Ain't much to see, though. Just the runnin' gears an' stuff. Everything else is gone. Burned up."

"What happened?"

"Nobody knows."

"What about the people that were on it?"

"Dead, I 'spect, or carried off. None of 'em have been found."

Thoughts tumbled over each other in Levi's mind. Should he shrug, pretend indifference, then find a later opportunity to return to examine the site? Should he take advantage of the opportunity to see it now? Maybe it would be best to just tell Wade who and what he really was.

As soon as the thought of revealing his identity passed through his mind, Levi felt again that chill of foreboding and decided against it. "I gotta see that," he said.

Wade reined off the road at once. "C'mon, then, I'll show you. This way."

They rode in silence, but Levi's eyes were darting everywhere. The ground was rocky. Rocks of all sizes jutted up through the ground at irregular intervals. Some of them would only have jostled a wagon. Others would have made it impossible to roll across, forcing any wagon to drive a tortuous path around them.

Clumps of short sage dotted the ground, as did larger clumps of yucca, known more commonly as soap weeds. Grass was plentiful, and ranged from the short wiry buffalo grass to taller varieties, including bunch grasses, with more bulk and less nourishment.

They rode across a low hill and into the hollow beyond it. The horses labored up the other side, bringing more questions to Levi's mind. The wagon train would have had to pick a very difficult and circuitous route to get very far in this terrain. It was just not possible for a normal team to pull a loaded covered wagon up the sides of these hills.

It was more than half a mile from the road when they found it. They sat together on the rim of the wide, shallow draw looking down on the scene of utter destruction. The blackened earth bore mute witness that the fire was not confined to the wagons themselves. The grass had burned over a wide circle to the east of the remains of the wagons, but had not burned west of them at all. "West wind," Levi muttered.

"What's that, Wink?" Wade asked.

Levi recovered quickly. "I just noticed that danged wind was in the west again when it happened."

"Whatd'ya mean?"

Levi nodded toward the blackened ruins. "The fire all went to the east till it burned itself out. Must've been kinda wet, too. It didn't burn very far."

"It's a wonder it didn't burn half of Nebraska."
Levi smiled tightly. "Let's ride down and take a closer look."
Wade shook his head. "There ain't nothin' to see. I looked

already."

Levi wasn't listening. He had already nudged his big buckskin gelding into a walk. He minced his way down the hill, not liking the smell of old fire that still hung in the air. He was halfway down the hill when Wade caught up.

"What do you want a closer look for? You got some interest in it?"

Levi shrugged. "Curious, I guess. What did you say burned 'em?"

"Nobody knows," Wade stated flatly.

"That don't make a bit o' sense," Levi responded.

Wade shrugged, not bothering to answer.
At the edge of the burned grass, Levi stopped his horse. He stepped off and dropped the reins. He walked toward the nearest wagon. His eyes took in everything. He saw the pattern of the fire, as it had reached out from each wagon. Seventeen small fires had licked across the ground eastward, until they all joined together to form one line of fire that burned to the rocky ground near the top of the next hill. There the sparse grass had offered less fuel, and it seemed to have died of its own accord.

"Must've been just a little bit wet," he muttered again.

"I reckon," Wade agreed absently.

Levi watched the ground intently as he walked. He saw the imprint of booted feet in the ashes and ignored them. He was more interested in tracks made before the fire, but he saw none yet. He was almost to the remains of the first wagon before he stopped. He bent down, watching the ground.

"What are you lookin' at?" Wade called.

"Just lookin'," Levi responded without turning around. The tracks he had spotted were made by two separate people. They were both small-heeled, pointed-toed tracks. They were made before the fire. Burned grass lay across the tracks, undisturbed since the fire.

"White men made them," Levi muttered. "Those are ridin' boots. Could be somebody from the wagon train, but not likely. Nobody but the scouts usually wear boots. Wagon train folks pertnear always wear them farmer type workin' boots."

"What?" Wade called. He had stayed out of the ashes and burned ground, following along as closely to Levi as he could without entering the burned area.

"Nothin'," Levi answered. "Just talkin' to myself."

"I thought it was only sheep herders who did that."

"That so? I didn't know they did. I thought they talked to their sheep."

"That's the first couple months. Then they talk to themselves. The fourth month they start answerin' themselves, too."

"That when they decide they're crazy?"

"Naw. They never do decide they're crazy. That's what makes it bad. It's okay to be crazy if you know you are. It's bein' crazy but not knowin' it that's bad."

"Then what do they do?"

That was obviously what Wade had been waiting for. He swept his hat off, held it against his chest, and looked melodramatically upward. "Then they just go ba-a-a-a-ack to Monta-a-a-ana," he said, making it sound like a sheep bleating as he said it.

Levi did not respond. All through the bantering he had never looked toward Wade, never stopped his minute inspection of the ground. He stopped as he arrived at the charred running gears of the first wagon. The heavy beams of the chassis were only partially burned. The iron braces, staves and supports were still attached, in many instances, to the blackened wood. The iron bands of the wheels were still in place. Some of the wood of the wheels and spokes had been burned. Other parts were intact.

The fire had left little. Levi frowned thoughtfully. He got down on all fours and smelled the ground beneath where the wagon had stood. Then he took some of the ashes and rubbed them between his thumb and fingers, then smelled his fingers.

"Coal oil," he confirmed.

"What's that?"

"Coal oil," Levi repeated louder. "They started the fire with coal oil."

"Who did?"

"Whoever burned the wagons."

"You mean the Indians?"

"If that's who burned the wagons," Levi responded. He was already moving toward the remnants of the next wagon.

"You gonna spend all day here?" Wade called. "Let's ride." Levi ignored the impatience or irritation tingeing Wade's voice. "I guess we wasn't in any big hurry. This fascinates me. I want to look this over."

He stopped abruptly as he neared the next wagon. Its ruins lay less than a hundred feet from the first one he had inspected. On the ground, almost against the charred tongue of the wagon, lay a burned portion of an arrow. He picked it up, looking at the arrowhead and the binding that attached it to the shaft.

"Shoshone," he said softly. Even as he said it, he felt that cold wind tingle his spine. He knew the Shoshone Indians. He knew Washakie, the great chief of the Shoshone, personally. He had spent several summers and one whole winter living with them. This was not something the Shoshoni would likely do. But the arrowhead was Shoshone.

He dropped it, and moved along. He checked the ground beneath the wagon as he had the first one. Again, the lingering, oily smell of kerosene was unmistakable. His frown deepened. He wheeled and returned to the first wagon. From the end of the wagon's charred tongue, he followed the tracks of the team that had pulled it. In spite of the fire, the time that had elapsed, and at least one substantial rain, he was able to track the team toward the unburned ground west of the ashes and debris.

"What you lookin' at now?" Wade asked as he caught up.

"Just wonderin' where they took the animals," Levi replied

absently as he continued his course.

"How can you tell?"

"Follow the tracks."

"I don't see no tracks."

"That's not too surprising. Your horse draggin' you so far still has your eyes full o' dirt, most likely. The trail's there, plain as day."

"I don't see no tracks."

"Right there. See? That's where they bunched them. Before they set the fires, they unhitched the horses and oxen both. They gathered all the other stock that was with the train, and bunched them all over here, upwind, where the fire wouldn't get at 'em'."

"I'll be danged. I can see where there was a bunch o' stock there all right. That even left tracks enough for me to see 'em. I gotta hand it to you, Wink. You're a real tracker."

Levi wheeled and strode back to the scene of the destruction. He went to the wagon he had just started inspecting, and took up where he had left off. In the ashes of the third wagon he found the remnants of two arrows. As he blew the ashes off of them, his frown deepened again. He went back to the second wagon and retrieved the arrow fragment he had thrown back on the ground. He stood still a long time, staring at the three arrowheads, and the broken charred shafts attached to them.

Wade finally overcame his apparent reluctance to walk through the ashes and stepped up beside him. "Now what you lookin' at?"

"Look at these," Levi said quietly. "Do you know anything about Indians?"

Wade shook his head. "Nope. I know they shoot arrows, and rifles when they can get them, and kill folks and take scalps. What else is there to know?"

Levi looked squarely at him for the first time during the conversation. "One of these arrows is Shoshone. One is Crow. The other one I don't recognize, but it's neither Shoshone nor Crow. Indians didn't do this at all."

Wade's face paled. "What are you talkin' about? Why wasn't it Indians?"

Three tribes wouldn't be on a war party together. Especially two of those. No Shoshoni would ever team up with a Crow for anything. They hate each other. Those arrows don't have anything to do with what happened to this wagon train."

"Well, if Indians didn't do it, who did? And why? And where did the arrows come from, then?"

"I don't know, but I know one thing. Whoever did this were white."

Wade looked sharply at Levi. "I don't know, Wink. I ain't sure how you can tell that. Anyway, how come you're so all-fired curious about this thing anyway?"

For another instant, Levi almost told him. Once again he chose to keep his own counsel instead.

"That's the trouble with the law," he told himself silently. "I can't even trust the man I'm riding with."

CHAPTER

"Ain't you done bein' curious yet?" Wade's impatience was approaching agitation. He kept walking away, as though to mount up and ride off. But each time, he seemed unable to stop watching.

"I've never seen anything like this in my life," Levi answered. He continued his careful search of the remains of each wagon in the ill-fated wagon train.

"Me neither, but I didn't spend the whole danged day lookin' at it," Wade complained. "Let's go."

Levi ignored the request. "Don't you wonder why they stayed all strung out?"

"What do you mean, Wink?"

Levi straightened from his examination of the ground beneath the twelfth wagon. "They didn't have any warning they were about to be attacked, or they'd have bunched up. They didn't make a circle of the wagons, or upset any to take cover behind. They didn't shoot any horses to get behind for cover. There's not one dead animal, or any sign they defended themselves, or fought back at all. There ain't one spent cartridge nowhere."

Wade looked back and forth along the string of burned remains. "Sure don't look that way, now that you mention it. Maybe they weren't killed. Maybe some sort of ghosts came along an' took 'em."

Levi shook his head. "They're strung out here, along the bottom of this draw, like they're goin' somewhere. They all stop, right in their tracks. Something happens to all the people. Then the animals are all herded over there, upwind. Then somebody poured coal oil all over all the wagons, then set them all on fire."

"Maybe it just caught fire. I 'spect they all had some coal oil in their wagons," Wade offered.

Levi nodded. "But it would have been in cans, or jugs. It wouldn't have been spread out like that. The cans and jugs were all tossed aside after they were emptied. See how many of 'em have a can or a jug layin' just a ways from what's left of the wagon?"

Wade shook his head. He pushed his hat back to the back of his head again. "You don't miss a thing, do you?"

I ain't paid to miss anything that obvious, Levi almost said. Instead, he changed in mid-sentence to… "I ain't paid to .. be no detective or anything, but if I was, I'd sure have a lot o' questions about this deal. Let's look some more."

He ignored Wade's look of utter frustration and irritation. The ashes of most of the wagons contained parts of trunks and wooden crates. There were many books, some ruined by the fire, others almost untouched. Those that weren't burned were well battered by the rains and the incessant wind.

Packets that had contained food of various kinds were strung about. The food was gone, except for some potatoes and onions. The remnants of the packaging bore witness to the scavenging of wild animals.

Things that were in tightly packed containers suffered the least from the fire. Few, if any, of the containers had been opened before everything was burned. The tight packing allowed the wind to blow out the fires before everything was consumed.

Levi examined wagon after wagon. All the while Wade became increasingly impatient. Finally, Wade rode off a ways and began target shooting at some bottles he gathered from the burned wagons.

At the fourteenth wagon, Levi called Wade. "Hey, Doc, come look at this. Some of the seat's still here that didn't burn. The driver was shot while he was still drivin' it."

"How can you tell that?"

"See that dark stain?" Levi pointed. "That's dried blood. And that hunk chipped out of the top edge of the back, and that hole in the back, are both from bullets. He was sittin' in the seat, drivin' his team, and got shot twice, at least, before he could move."

Wade said nothing. His eyes had lost their usual dance and sparkle. He paid no attention to the wagon seat Levi was pointing at. He looked off across country.

"Help me pick this up," Levi said.

"What for?"

"Just tryin' to satisfy that awful curiosity I got in me."

Wade made no effort to reach for the wagon seat. Instead, he said, "That kind of curiosity could get a man killed."

"Could be. On the other hand, it might have been not bein' curious enough that got these folks killed."

"Whatd'ya mean by that?"

"Nothing, really. Just thinkin'. Help me pick this up."

At Levi's insistence, they picked up the remains of the seat. Using the burned wreckage of the wagon as an indicator, they held it as nearly as possible to its original position. Levi looked at the direction of the bullet's path through the wood. "Top o' that hill," he said.

"It came from there?" Wade asked as they dropped the wagon seat.

"Low," Levi affirmed. "Somebody layin' in the grass, right about the top of that rise we came over."

"Bushwhacked, you mean?" Wade said.

"Looks that way."

"Why?"

"Robbery, maybe."

"Robbery?"

"Some folks carry a lot of money with 'em when they come west. They sell out their businesses or their farms, sell off all their stuff, and have a good chunk o' cash money. A lot of wagons are built with false bottoms to hide it. There was quite a bit in the fifth wagon back there."

"There was? You mean there still is?"

"Not now. Somebody found it, but not till after the wagons were burned. The ashes of that wagon had been gone through real careful."

"How do you know it was money?"

"They missed one piece. There was one double eagle still there."

He held out the gold coin in his open hand for Wade to see.

"You don't say! Gold! How come the robbers missed it?"

Levi shrugged. "Just didn't look long enough, I reckon, or else it wasn't what they were after. If it was done for robbery, they wouldn't have been apt to miss it, though, I wouldn't think. It was quite a while after the fire when somebody found it. It was most likely some cowboy that thought he'd struck it rich, but felt like a grave robber for gatherin' it up to keep, so he was hurryin'."

Levi waited for Wade to comment, but he did not. It was a glaring omission. Wade made no mention at all of the obvious fact that the possessions of the wagon train's occupants had been thoroughly rifled by people who came along after the fire, not before. Whatever the motive, Levi was positive it was not robbery. In fact, he would bet his life on it.

"Let's walk downwind a ways," he said.

Wade's exasperation and nervousness were becoming increasingly apparent. "Now what are you lookin' for?"

"Just to see what blew away. The way the wind blows in this country, there should be stuff hung up in the sage brush and scrub cedar and such for miles."

"Well I ain't walkin' no miles a-lookin'. My feet are already bellyachin' about trompin' around here. I'll go get the horses," Wade asserted emphatically.

Levi looked over the next wagon as he waited. It was essentially the same as the others. The remains of a trunk sat on the ground, its exterior burned away from around the tightly packed clothes within it. That clothing was sheltered enough by the wagon's remains that it remained in something of a stack, burned all around the edges. Enough of the fabric remained to see that it was expensive clothing. It appeared to have been nearly new.

He stooped down and picked up a dress from the top of the pile. It was badly charred along two sides, where it had been against the sides of the trunk. The rest of it was intact. Beneath it, on what was now the top of the stack, was an intricately lettered piece of needlepoint. On a beige background, trees and a small cottage had been embroidered.

The hills behind the house were low, allowing room for a lot of blue sky. Overlaid on the blue sky were the words, God Bless Our Home. It was hemmed at the top, with a wooden dowel through the loop of the hem. A piece of yarn was attached to both ends of the dowel, so it could be hung on the wall.

Levi looked quickly to see where Wade was. He was almost to the horses, still with his back turned. For reasons he did

not fully understand, Levi removed the dowel, folded the piece of needlework and slipped it inside his shirt.
He had completed his examination of the last wagon when Wade arrived with their horses. He walked to his saddlebags and put the portions of arrows he had picked up into them.

"How many arrows did you find, Wink?"

"Nine."

"You still say it wasn't Indians?"

"I'm sure of it. Those arrows are from at least four different tribes. Shoshone, Crow, Sioux, and one I don't know. A couple aren't from any tribe at all."

"What do you mean?"

They're old arrowheads somebody's found. They tied them to sticks, to try to make 'em look like arrows. They didn't know what they were doing. They weren't tied by Indians of any tribe. A seven-year-old boy, in any Indian tribe I know of, could have done it a whole lot better than they were done."

Wade opened his mouth to say something, then closed it. They had ridden several hundred yards before he spoke. "What're you lookin' for now?"

"Oh, papers, paper money, stuff like that, that might have blown away."

"What do you want them for? Oh, the money I understand right enough, but what do you want any of their papers for?"

Levi shrugged. "Still curious. This whole deal just doesn't make any sense at all. Papers might give us some idea of who they were, at least."

"What difference would that make?"

Levi just shrugged again. They did find a number of papers, parts of many letters, one marriage license, a poem half written, and one birth certificate. The marriage license was from Sioux City, Iowa. The birth certificate was from a hospital in Omaha, Nebraska. Although he had heard of birth certificates, it was the first one Levi had seen.

"Certificate of live birth. Timothy Eugene Wheeler," Levi read aloud. Then to himself he read, "Father: Eugene Phineas Wheeler. Mother: Esther Lois Sickleman Wheeler. Birth: legitimate. Birth weight..."

"What'cha readin', Wink?"

Levi looked up, folding the paper in two without reading the rest. "A birth certificate."

"What's a birth certificate?"

"It's a piece of paper that shows when and where someone was born, and who the parents are. Big cities back east have hospitals or midwives' places where women go to have their babies, instead of havin' them at home. When they do, they give them one of these."

"What for?"

"It shows who the parents are. Sometimes that's important to inherit property." Then Levi smiled. "I don't know. Maybe it's just so somebody can prove they were sure enough born."

"Sorta seems to like you could tell that, just by lookin'."

"Not always."

"Why not."

"Well now, take you for example. Just from lookin', a man could get up a real argument, whether you was born or just happened. Fact is, how can you prove that some ol' cow didn't just drop you out on a flat rock, so you hatched in the sun?"

Wade opened his mouth twice to offer a suitable rejoinder, but was obviously unable to think of one. Finally he abandoned the effort and chuckled, shaking his head.

As Wade turned away, Levi slipped the birth certificate into his shirt with the piece of needlepoint. He put the rest of the papers they had gathered into a saddle-bag.

I sure don't know why I don't trust you, Wade, Levi thought to himself.

That feeling in his gut told him he was right not to do so, though. More and more he was careful to keep Wade from getting behind him.

CHAPTER

"I got better things to do than scratch around in all these ashes and stuff. I guess I'll be ridin' on."

Levi paused from his search. When it had appeared he was about ready to ride away from the scene of the burned wagon train, he had turned back again. It was obvious the fact did not set well with Wade.

Levi's face was impassive. "You headin' on up to the W-W?"

"Yup, I reckon. If you want a ridin' job, ride on up an' I'll recommend you."

"You say it's close to the La Bonte Stage Station?"

Wade pushed his hat to the back of his head, then quickly grabbed it and pulled it down firmly again, as the renewed wind tugged at it. "Naw. It's way south and west o' the station. You'll cross La Bonte Crick three or four miles afore you reach the station, if you follow the road. Of course, if you follow the crick, you'll come to it eventually. If you want to go to the W-W, just follow the crick upstream. It's ten or twelve miles up, close to the edge o' the mountains.

Just follow the trail or the crick either one. You can't miss it."

Levi nodded absently. "I might be a few days. This deal with this wagon train just plumb fascinates me. I might ask around about it a while, just for curiosity."

"You gotta be about the most curious man I ever saw. Well, see ya, Wink." Wade raised a hand and wheeled his horse.

"Ride careful. Don't get hung up again," Levi called in response.

He stood where he was until the cowboy was out of sight. Then he sighed heavily. He had no idea why he felt such a relief at the other's departure. Maybe he'd just grown to like being alone. "Gettin' to be a reg'lar hermit," he muttered. He walked the entire length of the destroyed wagon train again. He studied the ground carefully, trying to sort out tracks made after the fire from those made before. Because of the fire, because of least one substantial rain since the disaster, there was not much he could learn.

He was convinced of one thing: He could not find the track of a single unshod horse, except three that were obviously colts, too young to be driven or ridden. "There ain't been an Indian that's even ridden past the place," he said aloud.

He walked back to where he had left his horse. Mounting, he turned toward the hill that lay between him and the stage road. As he passed the first wagon he had examined, his eye caught the shine of sun on metal. He dismounted abruptly. As he swung from his horse, and angry buzz whined past his ear. His foot touched the ground as he heard the rifle shot, borne on the wind. Without hesitation, Levi whipped his rifle from his saddle scabbard and flattened on the ground.

He crawled quickly to the scant cover afforded by the ruins of the wagon, scanning the horizon for the source of the shot. The wind had begun to blow steadily again, and its sound masked anything he might otherwise have heard. He saw nothing.

His horse was still looking toward the rim of the hill, but, even as he watched, the animal looked away. With a huff of breath, he began looking for grass to munch. He snorted at the burned smell of ashes that greeted the effort.

Levi lay without moving for several minutes. Once, he thought he heard hoofbeats, but he couldn't be certain. The wind made faint and distant sounds impossible to hear clearly. Finally he moved, cautiously, toward his horse. There was no response from the hill.

Using his horse for some measure of cover, he walked the animal in a circle, moving toward the brow of hill some distance from where he thought the shot had come. He reached the crown of the hill and crossed it without incident. Continuing the circle, he approached the crest of the hill from the other side. Almost at once he caught the reflection of the sun on a metal casing.

He dismounted and examined the ground. A bright brass casing lay where it had fallen in the grass. He bent to pick it up. "Thirty-thirty," he said aloud to the ceaseless wind. Scanning the traces of tracks by broken blades of grass and slight scuffs in the ground, he tracked the would-be bushwhacker back to where his horse had been left. His eyes followed the horse's trail back onto the stage road, where it was lost in the maze of tracks and hard earth.

"One shot and run quick," he muttered. "Wonder if he meant to get me, or just to discourage me from pokin' around so much?"

He returned to the brow of the hill from which the shot had come. The glint of sun on another piece of brass caught his eye. Stooping, he picked up a second brass casing. "Fifty caliber," he grunted. "That's a surprise."

He began at once a systematic search of the area. Within minutes he found places where three people had lain in the grass, well spaced along the length of the wagon train, firing down on it. He stood on the crest of the hill and surveyed the scene again. He suddenly raised his eyes and scanned the brow of the hill across the narrow draw.

"I wonder if there was some on that other hill too?" he asked aloud. "Do you suppose it was that well set up ahead of time?"

He mounted and rode quickly across the low ground and climbed the hill at the other side. Within thirty minutes he had found the site of three more riflemen, who had lain in wait for the ill-fated wagon train. Their traces in the ground were long gone, but they had not bothered to collect the spent brass casings extracted from their rifles. Levi catalogued in his mind the various calibers represented.

He suddenly remembered the metal the sun's reflection had revealed before. It had saved his life, causing him to dismount suddenly. He still didn't know what it was. He mounted his horse again and returned to the location.

It took him some time to find it this time. The sun's position had changed enough that it no longer reflected its light, but his memory was detailed and accurate. He knew within a circle of a yard where it had to be.

Even so, it was hard to spot. It was a two-inch broken section of gold watch chain. The end still had the fitting to attach it to a vest or trouser. He stood looking at it for a long moment, then dropped it into his pocket. Mounting, he rode back to the stage road.

The sun was near to setting by the time he covered the eight miles to La Bonte Creek. He crossed its clear, cold flow, then followed it upstream until he found a good camp site. There he staked out his horse to graze, fixed himself some supper, carefully put out his camp fire, and rolled into his blankets.

Thirty minutes later, when it was fully dark, he slipped silently out of his blankets. He rolled them up to make it appear he was still wrapped in them. Then he slipped quietly away from his camp site. With an extra blanket wrapped around him, he snuggled back against a scrub cedar tree and went to sleep.

He was awake and moving again just before sunup. He approached his camp site cautiously as the light brightened. Making a complete circle around it, he examined the ground with minute attention to detail.

The only tracks he found were from small nocturnal animals. Even those showed no signs of haste or fear. Satisfied, he strode to his blankets, retrieved his hat, pulled it down snugly on his head, and began to build a fire for breakfast. After breakfast he heated water over the small fire and shaved, using the large knife sheathed at his belt. When he had finished he stropped the knife blade on his boot top until it was once again sharp enough to satisfy him.

Within the hour he was back on the stage road, heading toward the La Bonte Stage Station. The wind was still blowing, but more softly than usual. The sun was bright, with only a few snow-white fleecy clouds to accent the impossible blue of the sky. The smell of sage floated on the wind. At the top of almost every hill he could see bunches of pronghorn antelope watching his passing. Once a lone, old and shaggy buffalo sauntered to a waterhole, as though blissfully unaware of the near annihilation his specie faced.

The day was too peaceful for thoughts of danger or intrigue. As Levi approached the station, he was completely relaxed. It was the last time for many years he would approach a strange place that carelessly. He shouldn't have this day. The corrals and a crude animal shelter were behind the main building. He rode toward them, around the edge of the hastily built station. The construction was mostly rock, gathered from the surrounding area. The spaces between the rocks were chinked with mud and dirt, making it appear more ramshackled than it really was. The windows were just blank openings, with buffalo hides tied back from them, that could be closed across them during inclement weather or against the winter's cold. The roof was made of pine and cedar poles, and the end of each was tied down with a heavy wire, anchored to something buried in the ground.

"Tied the wire to rocks and buried them in the ground," Levi told himself. "Got to, I s'pose, to keep that danged wind from blowin' the roof clean off."

The building was low, making the doorway too low for a normal man to enter without stooping slightly. As he rounded the back corner of the building, he continued to study its odd construction, paying attention to nothing else. He dismounted, still looking at the stage station. He heard a light scuff of booted feet and started to turn. As he did, lights and intense pain exploded without warning against the side of his head.

He staggered sideways from the force of the blow that seemed to have come from nowhere. He flailed his arms to catch his balance. His vision was too blurred from the impact to see anything except a red haze. He tried to focus his eyes, bringing his arms up to shield his face. A second blow, an instant behind the first, crashed into his stomach, driving the air from his lungs. Before he could even react, another slammed into his right kidney. Then other blows began to slam into him from all sides.

He tried to grab for his gun, but felt it pulled from his holster even as he reached for it. When his groping hand found the holster it was empty.

He reeled away, trying to escape from the attack, but every direction he turned, he was met with another smashing blow. The metallic taste of blood filled his mouth. The world spun in a dizzying red haze. Pain surged over and through him in wave after violent wave, radiating in excruciating spasms from every part of his body.

He was vaguely aware of blurred shapes around him, but he could see nothing clearly. Nobody spoke. He heard his horse snorting and prancing nervously, but he could identify no other sound. He tried to fight back, to swing, striking out blindly, but connected with nothing.

Another blow smashed into his face, but whatever hit him stayed there, pressing against his nose and mouth. It took seconds for him to realize it was the ground, and he that had fallen upon it. All he could see was that spinning red haze. Pain continued to rip at him from his ribs and groin, where booted feet continued to kick him unmercifully.

He tried to draw his legs up under himself, but was instantly rolled by another foot to his midsection. He gasped for air, and the pain of breathing brought waves of darkness up around him. The numberless blows continued. He felt an ear tear beneath a boot heel, almost as though it were being done to someone else. The roaring in his ears faded to a distant hum. Everything slowed until it all seemed to be happening in a dream, at impossibly slow speeds.

He knew in that moment that he was about to die. Unable to speak, he breathed in the sanctuary of his mind, *Lord Jesus, receive my spirit.*

The pain began to recede with the wave of blackness that was rapidly overwhelming him. The blood pouring from his mouth was choking him. Purely by instinct, he managed to roll onto his stomach and turn his head sideways, then the darkness swept over him. He gave up and sank into it, allowing it to blanket away the pain.

He did not hear the voice say, "That's enough."
He did not feel the sudden stopping of the kicks.
He did not see five men walk away without a word.
He did not know what they had done to his body. Yet. He would be most painfully aware of it tomorrow. If he were still alive. If he weren't, he would be turning summersaults in a world without pain.

CHAPTER

Pain washed over Levi from every direction. His eyes refused to focus. He thought his head was hanging downward, but he couldn't be sure. His body was moving and he felt nauseous. Intense agony swept over him in wave after wave. Darkness tried persistently to wash over him. He tried to fight it away. He tried to focus his eyes. He could not. He sank, instead, into that dark tide of oblivion.

He had no idea how much later it was that he again tried to open his eyes. They would not open. He felt hands touching him. Strong hands. Gentle hands. He felt warm water against his countless wounds. A trickle of cool water touched his lips. He tried to swallow, and choked. The water came again. He managed to swallow twice. The blessed cooling washed down his parched throat. Never had anything felt so grand! Cool wetness radiated through him. It reached his stomach, and glowed with refreshing cool moisture. He reached with his mouth blindly for more.

A strange voice said, "Not now. Not too much now." It was a deep and musical voice with a strange accent he had never heard. He tried to think about it. It was too much effort. The flood of darkness was rising again. It swept him away with its welcome tide of painlessness.

Some time later he was distantly aware of someone lifting his shoulders, pulling him to a semi-sitting position. It brought unbearable pain.

That strange voice said, "A little water now."

He fought upward through the turbid depths of the darkness that surrounded him, held him down, imprisoned him. He tried again to open his eyes. He could not. It felt like something was holding them shut.

He felt the touch of something cool and wet against his lips. He opened his mouth to a trickle of water. He swallowed, and felt again the ecstasy of the cooling flow down his throat and into his stomach. He swallowed greedily until it was taken away again.

He tried to reach for it. The effort sent excruciating pain erupting through his whole body at once. The pain felt like an explosion that sent shock waves clear to his toes. He groaned.

The same melodious voice said, "You must try to not too much move around. I think there is nothing that is broken, but you are hurt now, very much."

Levi tried to talk. The best he could do was whisper through grossly swollen lips, "Who are you?"

"Not now," that strange voice replied. "Now it is to sleep more that you need."

Levi sighed as consciousness slipped away. He awoke again, some time later, to an urgent call of nature. He tried to get to his feet. Waves of pain washed against him like raging floodwaters, forcing him back down. He gritted his teeth with the urgency of his need.

A pair of hands lifted him, supporting him, helping him to make it a few steps from the blankets he had been lying on. He couldn't open his eyes. He blindly groped for his trousers, before realizing he had none.

The strangely accented voice that was, somehow, familiar, spoke. "It is quite all right here. You may let it go."

The permission was not necessary. It was suddenly impossible to do otherwise. The sense of relief was intense. With the relief, however, the waves of pain and weakness returned. He did not remember returning to the blankets.

He only vaguely heard that strange, disembodied voice say, "It is as I was much afraid. There is much blood."

Levi had no idea how much time passed in the haze of pain and semi-consciousness. He was aware of somebody taking care of him. He was aware of being fed some sort of broth with flavors he did not recognize at all. When his need to relieve himself became overpowering, those strong hands were always there to support him, help him stagger those few steps away from his blankets, and to return again.

Finally, with constant effort, he managed to get one eye open enough to let in a thin shaft of light. The light stabbed at him, forcing the eye closed again. He kept trying. By the end of the day he was finally able to open both eyes to narrow slits.

The vision through those narrow apertures was so limited he wasn't able to distinguish more than general shapes and blurs. Darkness came to limit even that. He kept trying to move, to work the incredible soreness from his arms and legs. The pain was intense. It lanced through him with each breath, as though every rib was either broken or torn from its moorings. His groin was so swollen he could not bring his legs together. His head was bandaged, so he had no idea what damage lay beneath the wrappings. He knew it hurt.

The next day he was able to open his eyes enough to be able to see clearly, even though his field of vision was limited.

"You have eyes that open now."

He turned his head, grimacing at the pain even that slight effort cost him. His eyes focused on the source of the voice for the first time. He blinked. He closed his eyes tightly, then opened them again. Knowing he must be hallucinating, he tried to shake his head to clear it. The effort brought a wave of pain and dizziness instead.

That voice sounded again, in an exotically musical laugh. "Your eyes do not deceive you. I am not a dream or a vision of your injuries. My name is Bodharma."

Levi forced his eyes to open and focus again. A man stood above him, grinning broadly. His teeth gleamed like marble settings in a face of finely chiseled, dark bronze features His head was wrapped in some strange cloth that made him appear even taller than he was. His clothing was some sort of loose linen. Even his shoes were strange, looking more like moccasins, but with strange markings and decorations. Their toes curled upward, ending in a point that looped back downward toward the instep. A sash of bright blue linen was tied around his waist.

"You been taking care o' me?"

The man nodded vigorously and enthusiastically. "I brought you to this place quietly. I thought it might not, perhaps, be wise to take you inside to the place where you were attacked, even though it is a public house.

"Where are we?"

"It is a rather secluded place where it is not likely we will be discovered until you have had time to heal yourself. I have only used a fire at night, while it is shielded, so neither its glow nor its smoke would be able to be seen."

"What did you say your name was?"

"I am called Bodharma."

Levi started to ask more questions, then stopped. Instead he said, "My name's Levi. Levi Hill. Have you got a drink of water? I'm spittin' cotton."

Bodharma lifted a metal cup that was sitting on the ground, almost at his feet. Levi took it himself, sipping slowly. As he drank, the man spoke again.

"That is a strange expression, 'spitting cotton.' I have not heard it before. In any case, it is better than what you have been spitting," he said. "For much time you were spitting only blood."

"I got whupped up on pretty good, didn't I?"

He nodded vigorously again. "It is more than I have seen a man beaten and still live. They must hate you very much."

"Did you see who did it?"

"Only from some distance. I was riding from a small wadi behind the station of the stagecoach, on my horse. I saw five men ride away in a very large rush. Then I also saw you, lying on the ground, very much bleeding and very much hurt. I thought perhaps it would be a good thing to get you away from there, to see if you would live or die. I put you across my horse, and we came here. I brought also your horse with us. I do not believe that I was seen."

Levi digested the information for several minutes. When he had finished the water he set the empty cup on the ground. "How long have we been here?"

"It is the fifth day today."

Levi's eyes opened wider. "Five days?"

Bodharma nodded again. "It is the fifth day, this one that we have just begun. You were very near to death, my friend."

Another thought suddenly occurred to him. "Did you say you brought my horse?"

The man nodded again, that vigorous nod that seemed much too enthusiastic. "He is with my own horse, where they can eat. Your saddle and your things also, are here. I made the presumption that it was your gun and your knife that were lying upon the ground, and I have taken the liberty of bringing them with us also."

A sense of appreciation almost overwhelmed Levi. "I guess you thought of everything," he said.

"It is to be desired that you eat some of the things I have prepared, then perhaps to sleep again."

Levi took the plate of food that was handed to him. He did not recognize anything he was eating. He thought the meat might be venison, but it was seasoned in ways he had never tasted. It was chopped up into a finely minced mixture with, what he guessed, were roots, but he could not be sure of any of it. He was sure of two things: it was delicious, and he was hungry.

When he had eaten his fill he lay back on his blankets and was asleep again at once.

The seventh day, he dressed for the first time. His clothes felt loose and heavy. Bodharma had removed the bandage from his head that morning, examining the ear that had been torn almost off. He brought out a brightly polished piece of metal that allowed Levi to look at himself in its reflection. "Glad it's a metal mirror," he said. "That face'd bust it for sure, if it wasn't."

His face was swollen grotesquely. His eyes were puffy. His lips were much too large, cracked and discolored. His nose was swollen to at least twice its normal size. The whole of his face, from his eyebrows to his chin, was a deep purple. The ear that had been torn was red and swollen, but it was obviously healing back to his head.

"They did a real job on me, didn't they?" he said.

Bodharma laughed unexpectedly and uproariously. "You have been beaten nearly to death. You look upon your face and it is such that would cause an infant to cry. Your pains are many and over the whole of your body. But you admire the job they did in beating you as though it were a work of art!"

"Yeah, well, that doesn't hurt as much as thinkin' about how sore I am."

"Ah. It is to think of that which hurts less. That is not a bad thing. I was able to make your ear attach to the side of your head, and I straightened your nose so that it was not all over on the one side of your face as it was. Inside of it, I straightened things as much as I could do."

"At this point, I think you did a fine job."
He forced himself to walk a circle around their campsite several times. Each time he felt a little stronger. His hunger was a consuming and insatiable thing. He ate everything Bodharma prepared and wished for more.

By the next evening he was able to sit by the fire. He tried to think of a tactful way of satisfying his curiosity. He could not. Finally he decided to take the bull by the horns.

"I've never seen anybody like you. Where are you from?"

Bodharma laughed that lilting musical laugh again. "I have wondered how long you would contain your curiosity. It was most evident when you first began to be able to open your eyes that you thought you were dreaming when you looked upon me."

"It was a bit of a jar, all right," Levi admitted.

Bodharma laughed again, handing Levi a cup of tea. Levi took it gladly, fully aware of how much strength he had been drawing from that odd-tasting brew. The man stretched his tall frame out on the ground, folding his hands behind his head. He looked at the sky and talked.

"My name was not always Bodharma. I took the name at the time I came to your country. I am from a place that is called the Taklamakan, in the Kuen-lun Mountains. It is very, very much far away. It was necessary that I go away from there. A man who had become my friend told me much of this new country. He was a man of fine education and good family. He it is who has taught me to speak your language."

"He did a good job."

"Thank you. I am pleased that you think so. He helped me to come here, to this country. I have thought to travel to the place they call California. I am told there are many people there from many different lands, who have come there by sea. Perhaps I will not seem so strange there.

"Is Bodharma your family name?"

The man was silent for a long while. When he spoke, at last, there was an almost pensive note in his voice. "It is almost the name of one who is a legend among my people. He is the one who brought to my people a new way of defending themselves. It made me able to keep my life. It was not, however, enough for me to preserve the lives of the others. To use the name to which I was born, would be to invite a great trouble to follow me, even here. They would pursue me, and kill me, as they did my wife and my child and all the others. When I was able to leave, I chose to use as much of his name as I could do, without using that name myself, which is very much like sacred to me."

He fell into silence. A dozen questions tumbled over each other in Levi's mind. He thought it best not to ask any of them. He had already pried far too much into the life of another. If Bodharma wished to tell him any more, he would do so of his own accord.

He thought suddenly of the papers and things he had collected and put into his saddlebags. With a great effort he got up and walked to where Bodharma had stashed their gear. The papers and arrows were gone from his saddlebags He turned the matter over in his mind for a while. Then he turned back to Bodharma. "I had a couple things rolled up in my blankets instead of my saddlebags. Did you see them?"

Bodharma nodded. "There is a piece of paper and a very beautiful thing that is made to hang upon a wall, that was in your blankets. I placed it over there where is also your clothing and your guns."

Levi retrieved the two items and studied them. Then he remembered something else. He reached into his pocket and brought out the broken piece of watch chain. It wasn't much, but he had, at least, kept his attackers from getting everything.

His sleep that night was the closest to normal it had been since he was attacked. "I guess I'm gonna live after all," he murmured as he drifted into the soft shrouds of sleep. "Time'll tell whether that's a good thing or a bad one."

CHAPTER 7

"Your manner of dress is so strange."

Levi burst out laughing. Bodharma looked at him in obvious confusion. As soon as he could control himself, Levi obliged to explain.

It had been six weeks since the attack. His wounds had healed except for residual sore spots. His strength had returned, although not yet to its formidable level. They were readying to travel. For the first time since Bodharma had carried him to that hidden campsite, Levi was fully dressed. It was that, which sparked the comment from Bodharma. "You're the one that looks a mite outa place," Levi countered. "I look just like everybody else in the country. If we were to walk down a street together, I think you'd get the most stares."

"But even in the cities of your country, the people do not dress in the manner that you do," Bodharma insisted.

"Yeah, but out here they do," Levi replied. "It all has a purpose."

"Explain to me then, please, the purpose of the items, of the things you wear."

"All of them?"

"Oh, yes, please, if you would be so kind. I have such a very great curiosity about these things, and they seem so strange to me."

"About as strange as that turban looked the first time I saw you, I 'spect," Levi agreed. "Well, I ain't never tried to explain everything a cowboy wears, but I'll give it a shot." He pushed his hat to the back of his head and thought for a minute before he continued. "Let's start off from the ground up. Every cowboy wears boots, and they're built just right for ridin'. They're especially necessary if you're ridin' somethin' that might blow up with you."

"Blow up?"

"Yeah. That's a word we use for when a horse starts bucking. And most cowponies sorta like to do that, now and then."

"And the boot is a help for that?"

"Yeah, that's what I'm workin' on explainin'. The heel is high, and slung forward on the bottom. That's to keep it from goin' all the way through the stirrup. When your foot slides into the stirrup, the heel stops it. It's sloped, so if the horse bucks and the stirrup gets loose on the way back down, your foot won't slip clear through, or lose the stirrup."

"What would be the problem with your foot going through? That seems to me to be a very minor thing. Why could you not just pull it back again?"

"If the horse is buckin', you ain't got time. If you lose that stirrup, you can't use your feet to help you keep your balance, and stay in the saddle. If you buck off, and your foot's through the stirrup, you'll hang up, with that foot hooked in that stirrup so you can't pull it out. Then your horse will drag you to death, or kick your head to a pulp while you're floppin' around with your foot caught up in that stirrup."

Bodharma's eyes lit up. "Then it is even a matter of saving your life to have the very high heel with the forward slope. But does that not make it a very difficult thing to walk?"

Levi nodded. "It does that for a fact. That's why a cowboy will get on his horse to ride across the road. I keep a couple pair of moccasins in my saddlebags in case I have to walk somewhere."

"Moccasins. Ah, yes. That is the sort of shoe the ones called Indians who are not from India wear?"

"Yup. Now then, back to the boots. The boot's also got a pointed toe. That's so you can catch the far stirrup on the fly."

"Catch the far stirrup on a fly? I do not understand the stirrup being on an insect."

Levi sighed and thought a moment. "Well, to start with, 'on the fly,' don't mean the insect. That means real quick, while you're movin' fast. Sorta flyin' into the saddle, in a manner o' speakin'."

"Ah."

"Okay. Now picture getting on a horse that's about half busted or less. You know he's gonna break in two as soon as you fork 'im."

"Oh, please stop! I am terribly confused already. I do not understand 'half broke, or 'break in two,' or 'fork him.'"

Levi laughed. "This is gonna be harder'n I thought. Let me think a minute. Okay. When you teach a horse to let you ride im, that's called 'breakin' 'im.'"

"That means to train him to be ridden?"

"Yeah! Exactly. If he's well trained, then he's well broke. If he's only about half trained, that means you can ride 'im, but he's most likely gonna buck a little every time you get on. When you get on, you put one leg on each side of 'im, and that's called forkin' a bronc, or forkin' a horse."

"Ah, then I understand. Very well. You may proceed."

"Okay. Now, you're fixin' to get on a horse that's only about half busted..."

"Busted? What is having a bust about a horse?"

"Broke. Busted and broke mean the same thing."

"Oh. I had thought that busted was something that, well, that is, of the women, and... well, never mind. I understand now another meaning of the same word. Please continue."

Levi grinned. "Yeah, it is the same word, but a whole different meaning. Out here, busted and broke generally mean the same thing. Now, you're fixin' to get on this horse, but he's only about half bust... half broke. Okay? You know he's gonna buck. So you take the near rein and pull it up shorter than the other, make him turn his head toward you. You take the two reins together and you grab a handful of mane with the same hand. You stay right beside his front leg, so he can't reach you with his hind leg to kick you. Even though the near rein is pulled up shorter'n the other one, the far rein is tight enough he can't turn his head farther, so he can't reach you to bite you either. You take your right hand and twist the stirrup around, so your foot goes in the right way. Do you follow me so far?"

"Follow you?"

Levi rolled his eyes for a moment, then back to Bodharma. "That means, do you understand what I've described so far?"

"Oh. Certainly. That. Yes. Continue."

Levi suddenly realized Bodharma was acting out everything he was saying. He was standing now with his left hand up in the air as though he were holding the reins and mane, one foot in the air where the imaginary stirrup should be. With an enormous effort he avoided laughing. He continued. "Okay. Now you hold the reins and mane together tight, so when he starts to move, or buck, he has to do it in sort of a circle toward you. Having his head pulled around your way keeps him from jumping out from under you. If he jumps, it'll be under you instead. Then you move quick, and step into the saddle. But as you do, and your right foot comes over the top and down, you got to get it into that other stirrup quick. He ain't gonna stand there and wait for you to get settled in all comfortable, and tell him to go now, before he starts buckin'. He'll be breakin' in two before your rear end hits the saddle. The toe of the boot is pointed so it's a whole lot easier to hit that far stirrup on the first pass. That way you got that stirrup good and solid just as soon as you hit the saddle."

Bodharma thought the matter over, turning it in his mind at

length. He moved his hands and body this way and that, acting out the entire sequence of moves, before he spoke. Finally he nodded vigorously.

Then he said, "And the spurs you wear on the boots are to make the animal go faster?"

"Well, yeah, that's one use for 'em. They help you ride, too, though. Let's go back to this bronc we're talkin' about. When you hit the saddle, there are three things you do to be sure you can stay on."

With that, Levi reached out and put a hand on the swells of his saddle. "The humps out on the side of the front of the saddle are called 'swells.' You sort of hook your legs up here in this hollow spot just under 'em. Then you turn your toes out a ways, and hook your spurs into the cinch. Then you grab that saddle horn with your right hand, and hang on like crazy, to keep yourself pulled down into that saddle when he bucks. You got your spurs hooked in the cinch, your legs under the swells, and your hand on the nubbin', all helpin' you stay there."

"Oh, please, once again! I do not understand a nubbin. Is that a word that should be said 'nubbing'? And what is it? Levi laughed again. "No, that word ain't supposed to have the 'g' we tend to leave off the end o' words. It's properly called 'the nubbin.' That's just what we call the saddle horn. This part of the saddle."

"Ah. But I thought I was once told that it was on the saddle to attach a rope, in order to lead another horse or perhaps to drag a reluctant cow."

"It's used for that, or to take a dally when you rope somethin', but it's where it is so you can hang onto it when you need to. If it was just there to lead a pack horse with, they'd've put it around back, where it wouldn't be in the way, and where it wouldn't bust you in the gut, or somewhere worse, if you get on one you can't ride."

"Very well. Please continue."

"Well, that's the boots and spurs. Then the chaps are heavy leather, and they go on over your britches, and they keep you from gettin' your pants and your legs all tore up. That can happen if you're bustin' mossy-horns outa the brush, or a rope'll take the hide off of your leg in a big hurry if your rope runs across it with a critter on the other end."

"I am so very sorry. I feel like an infant, to be asking all the questions about what you are saying, but what is a 'mossy-horn'?"

"That's just a word that means some ol' cow that's kept herself hid so long in the brush that she's got moss growin' on her horns. She's like a wild animal, more'n she is like cattle. When you're on roundup and workin' cows and such, you gotta chase 'em through some pretty thick brush. If you don't have chaps, your legs will get all bloodied up, and your pants'll get torn to pieces. That's what the chaps protect you from."

"Then the part that is like a coat that does not have sleeves in it?"

"That's called a vest. It's to protect you from brush and to give you some protection from getting' horned, and such as that. It also helps keep you warm, when it ain't cold enough for your sheepskin. Not havin' arms in it makes it way easier to work in."

"And the thing about your neck?"

"It's called a neckerchief, or a bandanna. It protects the neck from cold and wind and dirt and such. When it's real dusty, or when you're ridin' drag…"

"Oh, please again! What is riding a drag?"

"It's not riding a drag. It's riding drag. That's ridin' at the back end, or the draggin' hind end, of a herd of cows on the move. It's real dusty, because all them cattle kick up a lot of dirt. When you're ridin' behind 'em, makin' sure none of 'em stray off, you get all that dirt and dust right in your face. Then you pull that neckerchief up over your mouth and nose, and it sorta filters out the dirt so you can breathe. That works in a blizzard too. When it's snowin' and blowin' hard enough, you can't face it and breathe without a neckerchief pulled up. Not to mention it keepin' your face from freezin' as fast."

"Ah, that makes very much sense. And that awfully large hat?"

"It has a purpose, just like the rest of it. It has a real wide brim to shade your face and neck. If you're caught out when it's cold enough you'll freeze your ears off, you can use your neckerchief or a piggin' string to tie the brim down over your ears. In the summertime, this sun out here bears down real good. The crown is high, to give your head room for a little air. And it's got to be big enough to hold enough water for your horse to drink."

"Excuse me! What? For your horse to drink?"

"Well, yeah. If you're crossin' a dry stretch, or if your source of water ain't big enough for a horse to get his nose into, he can't drink. So you pour water, from your canteen or whatever, into your hat, and you let him drink out of it. The same thing goes for oats, when you're on the move. A cowboy on the move always has a small bag of oats along. You can put some of 'em in your hat, and the horse can eat 'em outa there."

Bodharma laughed that long, musical laugh again. "That is so delightful a thing to hear! Never would I have thought of anything such as that. That you would do that, so that your horse could drink the water of your own canteen is... is... but keep telling me more. I must hear of these things."

"Another time, maybe. We gotta ride."

Bodharma's disappointment was evident, but he only shrugged. They were well packed and ready to leave. Levi watched the strange man mount his own horse. He did so smoothly and easily, even without stirrups. He rode only on a blanket across the horse, as an Indian would have done. His pack was secured to the horse's withers, in front of him.

"Where do we ride, my friend?"

"To the stage station."

Bodharma's eyebrows lifted, but his expression remained otherwise unchanged. "To the place where you were so very much less than welcome?"

Levi grinned. "I'm kinda over bein' sore. I thought I oughta see if I could try again. Anyway, I got you to carry me off and nurse me if I get whipped again."

Bodharma only frowned. "What is it that you wish to gain by returning to that place?"

"Well, somebody sure doesn't want me nosin' around about that wagon train. He took a pot shot at me, while I was still there. He musta been tailin' us, then stayed with me after

Doc left. He seems to've been keepin' tabs on where I was headin'. When I got here, he had a welcomin' committee all set up. Then they took all the stuff I'd picked up there, that I had in my saddle bags. The only sense I can make out of that is that he's tryin' to scare me off. Whoever it is, is tryin' to keep me from findin' out anything."

"You are known to be investigating that destruction?"

"Well, I tried to keep it under my hat, but it was pretty obvious I was way too interested in it. Somebody figured it out easy enough."

"Then the intention was not to kill you?"

"I'm plumb sure it wasn't. If they wanted to kill me, they'd've just stuck a bullet in me, as dumb and blind as I rode into that yard. No, I think they just wanted to tell me, in no uncertain terms, to go away and mind my own business."

"And why then do you not do so?"

Levi grinned. "Two reasons. First, there's the law. I got a job to do. But mostly, runnin' just ain't in my nature. If they want to get rid of me that bad, I just gotta know why." He sobered as he continued. "Besides, somebody blindsided me. Sooner or later I'm gonna find out who, and give him one more chance."

The sudden tickle of hairs lifting along the back of his neck convinced him he would indeed have that chance.

CHAPTER

"I must've rode in here sound asleep!"

The La Bonte Stage Station was not at all as Levi remembered it. The only thing he remembered accurately was the way the roof poles were guyed down, to keep the roof from blowing off in the ceaseless wind. He could not believe he had allowed himself to ride into a strange place as blindly as he had. He did not remember the houses east of the stage station. He did not recall seeing the signs that somebody expected this to be a town, one day. He didn't even remember noticing it was much more than just a stage station. In spite of its crude appearance, it was obvious to him now that the building housed both a saloon and a mercantile store. Behind the stage station was another rough building that opened onto a large corral behind it. It may well have served as a livery barn. Another long, open-sided building served as something of a shelter for horses, whose riders were in the store or saloon. A feed bunk and a water trough ran the length of the building, just in front of the hitching rail. Several horses were tied up in that shed. Most of them had the bridle bits out of their mouths, to allow them to eat and drink freely.

This time Levi rode in with his senses fully alert. The strap was unfastened from his Colt 45. He was ready for trouble. He and Bodharma tied their horses in the lean-to and entered the darkness of the low-ceilinged stage station, saloon and store.

"Hi. Can I help you?"

A sudden rush of pleasure coursed through Levi as he looked at the young woman who greeted them. She was no more than two inches over five feet tall. Her sandy hair was pulled back and tucked under a bandanna tied around her head. Her nose was small and slightly turned up. She exuded a sense of fresh, clean vibrancy that nearly took his breath away.

"May I help you?" Levi corrected with a grin.

"No, but I may help you," she retorted with a pert tilt of her head. "I may help you right back out that door if you only came in here to correct my grammar."

"I've never even met your grammer," Levi returned. "How could I correct her?"

"Oh, you are a smart one," she grinned. "I'll quit while you're ahead. What can I help you with?"

"We need a few dry goods, some ammunition, and my friend, Bodharma, here, would like some special tea from India. He's partial to it."

"Would he now! I've got the dry goods and ammunition, but I'm afraid I'll have to send an order out by stage for the tea. We should be able to have it here in, oh, say, two or three years. You do intend to pay for it in advance, of course?"

"Maybe we'll settle for some Arbuckle."

"Sorry. We don't have any coffee left till the next freight wagon comes. I've got some chicory though."

Levi made a face. "No thanks, too bitter for me. I'll just scrimp along with what I've got, and make it last a while." He continued to visit with her as they picked out the things they wanted. He found her surprisingly well educated, articulate, and thoroughly enjoyable to visit with. As she added up their bill, he decided to introduce himself. "Oh, by the way, my name's Levi Hill."

She surprised him by holding a hand out to him. He took it, and she shook hands with him as she replied, "I'm glad to meet you. I'm Cordelia O'Connor. It's nice to talk with somebody who's educated and has a sense of humor."

"Does your husband own the station?"
He was instantly sorry he had asked the question. A cloud darkened the dancing sunlight of her eyes. Her mouth thinned to a tight line. She sighed heavily, without being aware she had done so.

"I just work here," she said quietly. "My husband was killed. We had a homestead on upper La Bonte Creek."

"I'm really sorry," Levi asked. "I didn't know. How did he get killed?"

He could have kicked himself for opening his big mouth again without thinking, but she didn't seem to take offense at all. "He was shot. Nobody seems to know why, or by whom. He just didn't come home, so I went looking for him. He must have surprised some rustler, or some renegade

Indian, or something."

"I'm sorry," he said again. "So you got a job here?"

She looked around at the stacks of goods in the store. Levi's eyes followed hers. He noticed for the first time how perfectly organized and neat the store section of the building was. It stood in marked contrast to the disorderly clutter of the rest of the establishment.

Her eyes returned to him. "I like this country. I like its people, its open freedom, its newness. I didn't want to go back east. Butch Westfal bought my homestead rights from me, and put one of his hands on the place. He was very generous. He offered to help me go back east if I wanted to. When he found out I wanted to stay in the area, he got me this job. He even saw to it that I had a house to live in."

"He sounds like a good man."

She nodded. "Most of the people in this country are. That's one reason I like it so well. Even the rough and tumble sort are actually pretty decent inside."

"You aren't afraid to be alone, with all the men that stop in here at the saloon?"

She smiled. "No. I don't go into the saloon at all, of course. They know I am not that kind of woman. They respect me, and, I think, would protect me to the last man if they needed to. If there were ever a whisper that I was anything other than perfectly respectable, it would be a different matter, I'm sure."

On an impulse, he nonchalantly tossed out another question. "You wouldn't happen to know anything about the burnt wagon train, would you?"

Her eyes leaped up to meet his. She stared at him without a sound for several heartbeats. He could see her quickened pulse in the sudden veins appearing along the sides of her neck. "Why should you ask that?"

He thought of several evasive things to say, then decided against all of them. Deceit just gave him one more problem that kept getting in his way. If he was going to be working for the law, he was going to do so openly.

"I'm a range detective. I work for Pinkerton. I know it wasn't Indians. I thought you just might have heard something around the station."

Her eyes darted around the room before focusing intently on his own. He could see the shadow of fear lurking behind the calm exterior, but it did not sound in her voice. Her voice was soft enough only he could hear. "You might talk to the ferryman at Bridger's Crossing. It's on the Platte, about five miles downstream. But be careful."

In a louder voice she said, "Will that be all for you?"

He took a cue from her and adopted his former, more flippant demeanor. "Well, that'll be enough for now, I guess. If I buy everything I need today, I won't have an excuse to come back and see you tomorrow."

In a quiet voice, as they gathered their things, he said, "Thank you. Mind if I stop back in a day or two?"

His heart almost skipped a beat as she smiled at him. She replied, "I'd like that."

During the whole of the time, Bodharma had not said a word. He had seemed almost afraid of Cordelia, and avoided all eye contact with her. They picked up their purchases and returned to the yard.

By the time they had integrated their purchases into their other supplies, however, several men had assembled in the yard. Levi spoke softly to his companion, about whom he suddenly realized he still did not know a great deal. "Looks like we got a bit of a problem. Can you fight?"

Bodharma grinned broadly. "It is perhaps I who should be asking the question of you," he said quietly. "You did not appear to fend so well for yourself the last time you were here."

Levi flushed hotly. "They blind-sided me. I didn't come in asleep this time. How many of 'em do you want?"

"All of them, please."

"What? It looks like about five or six that are itchin' for a fight."

"That will be most satisfactory, I think. I will ask you to please allow me to deal with them. I will ask only that you will not allow anyone to slay me with a firearm while I am occupied with the others."

Levi opened his mouth to protest, but Bodharma had already turned his horse and was leading him toward the cluster of men who had gathered. As they approached the group, one man stepped out in front.

"What kind o' tin-horn get-up is that you're a-wearin'?" he asked. "It looks like some o' them fancy pyjamas I read about rich folks back east a-wearin'. You aimin' to go to bed?"

A chorus of rough laughter from the assembled group responded.

The musical cadence of Bodharma's overly refined response created an exaggerated contrast. "I wish only to pass unhindered," he said. "Please stand aside and allow me to do so peacefully."

There was just an instant of surprise as the quiet assurance of his voice caught them off guard. They were not daunted for long.

The self-appointed leader spoke again. "You can pass unhindered right on outa this territory. We don't want any dirty foreigners traipsin' around here, stinkin' up the country."

Bodharma smiled unexpectedly. "Ah. No foreigners. Then, I must assume that you are all native to this country. Does that mean you are all what are called Indians?"

Again there was an instant's disbelief, absorbed in silence. Then five of the six men began to talk at once, loudly and angrily, as they advanced on Bodharma.

The broad grin never left the dark man's face. He stepped away from his horse, letting the reins drop to the ground. Levi also stepped away from his horse, where he could keep all of them in his field of vision.

As the men advanced, they formed a rough semi-circle, so Bodharma was half surrounded as they approached. When they were all within about a yard of him, he acted. He lifted one foot and spun, catching the man on his right directly on the side of the head. The blow was so hard the man literally cartwheeled in the air, before crumpling to the ground. He had not yet hit the ground when Bodharma buried his extended fingers, upward from the stomach, under the rib cage of the second man, sending him into a doubled paroxysm of convulsing effort to catch his breath.

A chopping blow from the edge of one open hand, delivered to the side of the neck, dropped a third man like a pole-axed steer. The fourth man met a foot that caught him just under the chin and lifted his feet clear of the ground. Levi never even saw the blow that felled the fifth man. He simply flopped on the ground, thrashing violently and holding his throat. Less than five seconds had elapsed.

The sudden silence was shattered by a single shot. The sixth man, who had hung back from advancing with the others, took a step backward. His gun slipped from his fingers and hit the dirt with a soft thud. He dropped to his knees, then toppled forward and lay without moving.

Bodharma turned to look at Levi, who stood there with his gun in his hand. "He was fixin' to blind-side you a bit permanently," Levi explained. "Do you think maybe you killed them fellas?"

"No, I think not. Well, only the one, perhaps, if his throat swells too much he will not be able to breathe again. I think I did not hit him quite that hard, though. It would be perhaps a good thing that we leave this place?" Bodharma asked, still grinning broadly.

Levi really wanted to ask Cordelia a couple of questions, including the identity of the men who had attacked them. He wanted to know who they rode for. He wanted to know if she thought they had any connection to the burnt wagon train. He also knew if he returned to ask her those questions, it would appear she was helping hm. If his growing suspicions were right, that would put her in great danger. "Seems like it might at that," Levi agreed.

He addressed the half-dozen people who had emptied out of the saloon to watch the fight. "You fellows saw what happened. It was all fair and square, till that guy tried to shoot an unarmed man."

He indicated the prone figure of the dead gunman as he spoke. There was a quiet murmur of agreement among the watchers.

Levi walked to the dead man. He grabbed him by a shoulder and turned him over. One arm flopped outward as he turned. His hand lay, palm up, on the ground. Levi spotted a gold watch chain tied to his trousers with a knot. The other end disappeared into his watch pocket. He knelt and pulled on the chain. An intricately engraved gold watch emerged.

Levi untied the knot that secured the dainty chain to the coarse trousers. Reaching into his own pocket, he pulled out the fragment of watch chain he had found at the site of the burnt wagon train. They matched perfectly.

He looked around the cluster of onlookers. He singled out the bartender. "You're a witness. I'm taking this man's watch to its rightful owner. My name's Levi Hill. I'm a Pinkerton range detective."

He did not miss the reaction that announcement created, even though it was instantly stifled. "You can see to buryin' this man, too," he added.

The bartender shrugged. "Let his own outfit bury him, when they come around."

Grinning, Levi mounted. As he and Bodharma headed down the road, he said, "How did you do that? I ain't never seen anyone fight like that."

Bodharma's grin had vanished. He spoke clearly and softly. "It is the thing that was taught to my people by the one whose name I attempt to honor. Perhaps, if we are privileged to ride together for a while, I may teach you."

"That'd sure be worth learnin'," Levi replied. "Especially if I aim to spend my life workin' for the law. That was really somethin'."

CHAPTER

"Howdy, Doc."

Wade jumped violently at the voice. He whirled, hand dropping to his gun. He recognized Levi. His hand hung there, just above his gun butt. He swallowed hard, his Adam's apple bobbing rapidly.

Levi remained relaxed on his horse. The strap was unfastened from his 45. His hand lay on his thigh, inches from it, waiting to see what the cowboy would do.

Wade quickly rejected any thought of drawing. He had watched Levi's daily practice, during the few days they had ridden together. He knew how incredible fast the man was with a gun. He slowly moved his hand back to his vest, brushing idly at its front.

"Uh, hi there, Wink. You startled me. Matter of fact, you just about scared the pants off me. I didn't hear you ride up."

"Pants are probably about due for a change anyway. I was just ridin' by."

"I heard you wasn't ridin' alone. Where's that funny lookin' fella they said was ridin' with you?"

"We split up for a few days. By the way, my name's not really Wink."

"That so?"

"The name's Levi Hill. I work for Pinkerton."

Wade swallowed hard again. He had to make two efforts at speech to get the words to come out at a normal pitch. "That, uh, ahem, that how come you was pokin' around that burnt wagon train so hard?"

"Uh huh. It's my job to find out what happened. Who does a man called Schally ride for?"

"What? Who? Schally? Oh, him. I heard you killed him. Whatd'ya wanta know that for?"

"He was one of the guys that killed the people in that wagon train, or else one that went through their stuff and stole what he could find."

"What? Schally was? Why do you say that?"

"He had a watch that came from there. I found the broken piece of the watch chain by one of the wagons. He was wearin' the rest of it."

Wade's face paled perceptibly. "You, you don't say! Now who'd've thought it! He must've just been pokin' around there and found it or somethin'. You reckon?"

Levi didn't think it was that way at all, but he had no proof, yet. He decided it was best to let it ride that way. "Who did Schally ride for?"

"Why, he, uh, he rode for the W-W part of the time. I don't guess he has for a while, though. No, I guess he ain't rode for the W-W for quite a while, come to think of it. Why?"

"Just wonderin'. What's goin' on here?"

"Oh, uh, this here's the Wilson homestead. Sandy Wilson, he done got hisself killed a little while back. Westfal, he went and bought out her homestead claim, and give the widow a bunch of money so she could go back east to where her folks live. He sent me and a couple of the boys to help her load her stuff up and take her to Cheyenne."

Levi pondered the information as he looked the place over. The house was built mostly of rock. The roof was supported with pine poles for rafters, with some sort of lumber on top of the poles. It was topped with sod. The windows were of oiled paper. The door was a heavy buffalo hide.

"Don't look like too prosperous a place," Levi suggested.

"It's a hardscrabble outfit for sure," Wade agreed. "They wasn't makin' it at all, but Sandy was a stubborn sort. He figured sooner or later they'd be able to make it. Westfal offered to buy him out twice, but he didn't want to sell."

"Why would Westfal want it?"

"Water. Bottomland. The homesteaders tie up the land along the crick, and that ties up all the winter range. If Westfal ain't got winter range, he's outa business. He's got some of his hands provin' up on a few places, so he can buy it from 'em as soon as they get their deed. He buys out other homesteaders as soon as they figure out they can't make it out here on a quarter section."

"A hundred and sixty acres ain't enough to make a livin' on in this country, that's for sure."

Wade gave a short laugh. "You can't tell these Missouri and Illinois sodbusters that, though. Not till they starve out. Of course, by then they got the ground all tore up so it'll run to weeds or blow away. Then they start stealin' calves to eat, or to sell, just to keep their families alive. Worst thing Lincoln ever did, signin' that Homestead act. At least Buchanan had sense enough to veto it."

"I guess it's a good thing in some places," Levi offered.

"In a pig's ear it is!" Wade explained. "All it does is give all sorts of people high ideas about how they can come out west and just take any land they want. They take it away from the people that fought the blizzards and the drouths and Indians and the rustlers and everything else for it. They just take away the best chunks of it from 'em, and them not able to do a dang-blasted thing to keep 'em from doin' it, till they've already ruined the land, and poisoned the crick, and killed off all the game, and, and… No sir, it ain't no good thing, no place, no time, and I'll whip the man that says it is!"

Levi was taken aback by the vehemence of the sudden display. He still hadn't thought of a suitable answer when Wade spoke again.

"Anyway, I got work to do. You can just ride on along, Wink Lee, or Levi Hill, or whatever your name is today."

Just then a young woman walked out of the house with an armful of things and put them in the wagon. "I think this is the last of it. I… Oh! I'm sorry. I didn't see you had company."

She looked at Levi, then back at Wade's obvious anger. "I'm sorry," she said again. "Am I interrupting something?"

"No Ma'am," Wade said too quickly. "This here's Levi Hill, or so he says today. He was just leavin'."

Levi made no move to ride on. Instead he removed his hat. "Mrs. Wilson. I just heard about your husband. I'm very sorry."

Her eyes instantly filled with tears, but none spilled over. "Thank you," she said softly. "It was one of those things."

"How did it happen?" Levi asked, in that same soft voice.

Wade stiffened as he asked the question. Levi felt the cowboy's glare burning into him, but he ignored it. The woman's attitude made it clear she regarded the question as one of concern, rather than prying.

She sighed heavily. "I don't really know. The horses must have run away with him. They probably spooked at a rattlesnake or something. He had just started breaking up the sod, so he could plant a crop. He didn't come in for supper. Then the horses came in without him, dragging the plow, upside down. I went out to look for him. He was lying at the edge of the furrow. I could see where the horses had spooked and run, with the plow bouncing along. He was lying by a rock that he must have hit his head on, when he fell."

"I'm awfully sorry," Levi said again.

She sighed again, then spoke to Wade. "I'll go get Sarah, and I think we'll be ready."

As soon as she was out of earshot, Wade whirled on Levi. He spoke swiftly and vehemently, the veins standing out on his neck. "Now what did you have to go and do that for? Don't you think she feels bad enough without havin' to tell some stranger all about it, all over again?"

"It helps to talk about it," Levi replied.

"Helps you maybe."

Levi shook his head. "No, it helps her. She needs to be able to talk about it. How come Westfal's helpin' her?"

Wade shrugged. "That's Butch. He'll help anybody that needs help. If you was to try to take somethin' from him, he'd tear you apart. But if you ask for it, or if he thinks you need it, he'll just up an' give it to you. If it was up to me, I'd have shrugged my shoulders and said the dumb sodbuster got what was comin' to 'im, and let it go at that."

"You takin' the widow all the way to Cheyenne?"

Wade nodded. "Boss's orders. He wants to be sure she makes it okay, and gets her stuff all the way there without no trouble."

"Good of 'im," Levi observed.

"Like I say, that's Butch. Now, if you was fixin' to leave, don't let me keep you."

Levi smiled tightly and nodded. He pulled his hat down firmly and turned his horse away. He didn't like the tingling of his spine that continued until he was well out of rifle range, but he refused to do anything other than ride tall in the saddle. He heaved a big sigh of relief, though, as soon as a rise of ground intervened.

Less than a quarter-mile later, he encountered another homestead. There was no sign of life. The house was little more than a stack of rocks with a hasty roof thrown over it. A small corral and an even smaller lean-to provided the only evidence of expected animal life. There was a broken table and one chair in the house. There was no door and no windows, only gaping openings where a door and windows should be. The grass in the yard wasn't even matted down. "I guess that must be one of the places filed on by one of Westfal's hands," Levi told his horse.

The horse evidently agreed. He tossed his head twice at the sound of the voice, but showed no interest in stopping at the sham of a homestead.

A little farther up the creek they encountered another place, almost identical. The place beyond that one looked as if it had been lived in for a while, but it, too, was vacant.

The next place was considerably different. It had a house that was built with care, and looked snug against the weather. The corral was large, and solid enough to hold either cattle or horses. There was real glass in the house's four windows. A front door of milled lumber fitted tightly into its frame. A trail of smoke rose from the stovepipe that poked through the sod roof.

"Now this looks like a real homestead," Levi told his ever-attentive horse, who bobbed his head in total agreement.

"Let's see who lives here."

"Hello the house," he called, as he rode into the yard.

The door opened. "Hello yourself," the man replied. "Get down and come in. You're just in time for a bait of grub, if you're hungry."

"You got plenty?"

"If I don't, I'll rustle up some more. I fixed more than I can eat anyhow, and I hate to feed it to the dogs. They're too fat already."

"Well, I don't see how I can turn down a chance to help your dogs lose a little fat," Levi grinned.

"There's water in the trough if you want to let your horse wet his whistle."

"Well, I'll give him some, but it won't help. He can't whistle nohow," Levi replied with an overly serious expression. "I been tryin' to teach him Yankee Doodle for months, and all he does is snort."

"That so?" the man replied with equal seriousness. "You don't s'pose you got sold some rebel horse, do you? Have you tried gettin' him to whistle Dixie instead?"

"I'm afraid to," Levi said with no hesitation. "The last time I tried to teach him how it went, I got shot at before I'd whistled half way through it to show him how it went. I figured this must be Yankee country."

The man grinned broadly and held out his hand. "My name's Buck Rimmer. I ride for the W-W."

"Levi Hill," Levi replied, taking the man's hand. The grip was strong and solid. He looked at the man's honest, open face and liked him at once. "You ride for Westfal, huh? I thought this place looked like it was built to be permanent."

"It is, for a fact," Buck agreed. "A family from Iowa homesteaded it. They had two sons, pertnear growed up. They built real well."

"What happened to them?"

"Aw, they decided they couldn't make it on a hundred sixty acres. Then the two boys, they filed on the two chunks just down the crick, but they didn't have no intention o' livin' there. Anyway, Westfal convinced 'em they wasn't gonna make it, and bought 'em out."

"I saw the two places down the crick," Levi replied. "It looked like something thrown up to satisfy the government, not to live in."

"That's right, for a fact. Westfal was pretty generous with 'em, the way I hear it. Anyway, I'm fixin' to get married this fall, so Westfal offered to let me finish provin' up on this place, then he'll let us live here as long as I work for him. I got my own brand. He's gonna let me run some of my own cattle on his range, as I can accumulate 'em. Sooner or later I'll have a herd built up, then we can find us a ranch of our own."

"Nice setup. Westfal must be a good man to ride for."

"The best. He'd give you the shirt off his back, if he thought you needed it. Oh, he's a hard man, I guess, but he's fair. He works the daylights out of us. There ain't no lazy hands on his place. But if you do your job, he'll be fair an' generous, and he'll back you to the hilt."

There was little conversation during the meal. When they were finished, they shared idle range talk for a while. Then Levi thanked him and left. He continued to follow the creek westward, ever nearer the looming mountains of the Laramie Range. He passed the abandoned homestead he guessed must have been the O'Connors', from Cordelia's description. He continued to climb closer to the mountains. The increased altitude was evident in the thinning clarity of the air. The constant vexation of the wind, so much a problem a few miles east, seemed a thing of the past.

He rode past three more homesteads, all empty. Then a distance of three miles bore no evidence of any such activity. Finally, he came into sight of the ranch's headquarters. When he topped a rise in the road and saw it, he stopped abruptly to take it in.

A jagged cliff of reddish-brown rock rose high into the sky, forming a backdrop for one of the most perfect building sites Levi could remember seeing. A spume of white water cascaded down the face of the cliff, forming the beginnings of La Bonte Creek. The slopes that formed a semicircle against the background of mountains were heavily forested with pine and spruce, with the darker green of occasional cedars mingled in.

The ranch house stood just below the crest of a gentle rise. It was built of carefully trimmed logs, with a broad covered porch across the whole of the front. The roof sloped up steeply to prevent build-up of snow. The windows were made of real glass, with twelve panes of glass in each window. The door even had a single pane of glass in it. It exuded a sense of warmth and security that reached out to Levi from the three hundred yards' distance.

Quite a bit below, and about a hundred yards from the house, La Bonte Creek meandered by. From the vantage point of the house Levi was positive he would be able to see the deeper pools where trout would splash and waterfowl would swim. It was a picture of paradise.

Beside and a little behind the house, the bunkhouse looked just as solidly built. There were two smaller houses in the yard, a cook house, a couple of other buildings whose use was not immediately apparent, and a huge horse barn back closer to the cliff. The entire site was located just far enough from the cliff to keep the cascade of water from being too noisy. It could be heard, if you listened, providing a soft reassurance of normalcy, but its sound was not intrusive. "That place is a dream!" Levi breathed. "I'll bet you two to one they got a root cellar into that hill behind the house, that opens right into the house, so they don't even have to go outside to get into it."

As he sat there, drinking in the perfection of the scene, the blows of a blacksmith's hammer on the anvil drifted faintly on the breeze. "Even got his own blacksmith!" Levi marveled. "I sure hope I don't have to end up standing against the man that's built all this."

CHAPTER 10

The strap was off the hammer of his Colt. His horse walked steadily forward. His hand rested lightly on his thigh, inches from the gun butt. His eyes darted from building to building, from rock to rock.

A cowboy stepped out of the cookhouse and spotted him. He stopped, then turned toward the house. Levi could hear his voice carry on the light air, even though he was still two hundred yards from the house.

"Hey Butch! Company comin'."

The cowboy turned and continued on his way to wherever he had been going. Levi's attention was diverted to the main house as the front door opened.

A man walked out onto the front porch, pulling his hat down snugly onto his forehead. He stepped to the front of the porch, just by the wide steps. He shoved the fingers of both hands into the front pockets of his pants and stood patiently.

Levi took stock of the worn Colt .45 tied down on the man's

thigh. He noted the broad, strong shoulders and square jaw. He was close enough he thought he could see a trace of gray in the man's hair, between his ears and his hat. The man had a match stuck in one corner of his mouth. His face was open and honestly curious, but betrayed no other expression. As Levi rode up to the porch, he pushed his own hat to the back of his head. "Howdy," he said.

"Afternoon," the man replied pleasantly. "Nice day."

"Nice place, too," Levi responded. "It looks like something out of a picture book."

"Thanks," the rancher replied. "I'm sorta proud of it."

"You'd be Butch Westfal?"

"That I would."

"My name's Levi Hill. I ride for Pinkerton. I wonder if I could talk at you some."

"I've heard of Pinkerton. Detective outfit, ain't it? Sure. Get down and come in." He took a quarter turn toward the yard and called out in a voice that could have been heard a half-mile down the mountain, "Gimpy! Come take care of this man's horse for him."

He turned back to Levi. "You can just drop the reins. Gimpy'll put 'im up and give 'im a little bait of grain and water. Good-lookin' horse."

"Much obliged," Levi replied, following the rancher who had turned back into the house.

As he stepped into the relatively dim light of the interior, he almost gasped. The house bore an opulence that surpassed even that of the Rudabaugh place, where he had been raised. The parlor into which he had just stepped was spacious. French doors, with their dozen small panes of glass, stood open into the front room. The front room was carpeted with a thick wool rug that reached nearly to all four walls. The rug's primary color was deep wine, with a pattern woven into it of turquoise and gold.

Three sofas ranged before a huge fireplace. They were overstuffed, looking like dark leather clouds to sink into. Polished wooden arms and legs were the perfect complement to the leather, giving it stability and warmth. Several chairs of the same style were scattered randomly. A huge roll-top desk stood in one corner.

A large picture of a man and woman standing in a harvest field, heads bowed in prayer, dominated one wall. Several needlepoint pieces were hung about, giving it just the right touch of hominess. Rich draperies hung at the windows. The wine of their velvet was a perfect match for that in the carpet. Behind the draperies, lacy white curtains graced the windows, gently muting the outside view.

One window was an exception. The window directly in front of one large chair had the curtains tied back with lacy bows. The clear view through the window was precisely what Levi had imagined, looking up at the house from below. His eyes were drawn as if by a magnet to the view through that window. As if on cue, a pair of mallards descended and lit on a quiet pool of La Bonte Creek. The whole scene overwhelmed him so completely he just stood there, unable to move or speak. Finally, he said, "That must be just about what the Garden of Eden looked like," he breathed.

"It's what the whole world could've looked like if it wasn't for mankind's determination to sin," Westfal agreed.

Levi continued to stare in awed wonder. The lilting notes of "Fur Elise" suddenly emanated from a piano in an adjoining sunroom. His lower jaw dropped as he listened to the beauty of the music.

Westfal's voice broke the spell. "That's my daughter. We hauled that piano clear out here from Kansas City so my wife could teach her to play."

"Clear from Kansas City!" Levi echoed.

"You from around here?" Westfal intruded into his amazement again.

Levi finally brought himself around, remembering who he was and why he was here. "Sorry. I'm gawkin' like a school kid," he grinned. "This is the finest place I've seen. It's even nicer than Stubby and Eleanor's."

The rancher's eyebrows shot up. "Stubby and Eleanor! Rudabaugh?"

It was Levi's turn to betray surprise. "Yeah. You know 'em?"

"Know 'em! My wife growed up with Eleanor down in Texas. Haven't seen 'em for years, though. You wouldn't, by any chance, happen to be that kid they raised would you? The one they found, that survived the Indian massacre?"

Levi nodded. "That's me."

Westfal pressed the issue. "Are you the one that went after them Indians that took Myra, and brought her back?"

Levi nodded. His lips were thin and his eyes clouded at the memories. "Jim Keller and I," he said.

"Fine piece of work," Westfal said with feeling. "Even if you couldn't save her baby, it was a fine piece of work. I'd have bet my ranch you'd never be able to do it, that she was just gone for good. That's been the talk of the country ever since."

Levi was increasingly uncomfortable. He tried to think of something to say, and nothing whatever came to mind. He just stood there, hat in hand, while Westfal looked him over admiringly.

It was the rancher who finally realized how awkward it was for Levi. "Well," he said a little too loudly, "come on in here and sit down. I'll holler at my wife. She'll want to know all about how Eleanor is, and whether Keller got around to marryin' Myra yet, and everything else you know. You'd best get set, though. She'll ask you more questions in the next five minutes than you can answer in thirty."

Levi opened his mouth to protest, but the rancher was already gone. He was still standing there, hat in hand, when the rancher returned with a woman slightly younger than himself. Also accompanying them was the most beautiful girl Levi had ever seen.

"Levi Hill, I'd like you to meet my wife, Helen, and my daughter, Victoria. Ladies, this here's Levi Hill. He's Stubby and Eleanor's kid, that they raised."

Helen's eyes lit up at once. "Why, Levi, I'm delighted to meet you. I've heard so much about you. Do come in and sit down. How is Eleanor? Did Myra and Jim get married yet? I do hope she doesn't grieve too long for her husband and the baby. Oh, that was so awful! I'm so grateful you were able to rescue her at least. Are you here alone? Everything's okay at home, isn't it? Are you going to be able to stay long?"

Levi scarcely heard the flood of words from the rancher's wife. His eyes were filled to capacity with the beauty of Victoria. He skin was flawlessly smooth. Her eyes were large and dark, framed by cascades of dark brown hair that dropped in ringlets to her shoulders. She was less than two inches shorter than his own five-foot-seven, and moved with a smooth grace that was both feminine and strongly self-assured.

Victoria held out her hand to Levi. "Levi, I've heard about you. In fact, I've heard so much about you, I'm surprised that you're just a real human being. Hi."

He took her hand and was surprised at the quick strength of her grip. Levi's own voice sounded stiff and formal to himself. "Victoria, I'm pleased to meet you," he said.

"You'll stick around for a bite of supper, won't you?" Westfal said, more as a statement than a question. "You'll be stayin' in the guest room while you're here too."

"Please come in and sit down," Helen said. "You three can visit while I finish getting supper ready."

"I'll take your hat," Victoria said. "Do you want to take your gun off too? I'll hang it with your hat."

Alarm sprang up wildly in Levi at the thought of handing over his gun, but he saw the ease with which Westfal removed his own and handed it to Victoria. He did the same, but the action left him feeling naked and vulnerable. He soon lost the sense of danger, engrossed in conversation with the rancher and his daughter. From time to time Helen stepped in from the kitchen and joined in for a few minutes, but Levi hardly noticed. They talked of the Rudabaughs, the rescue of Myra, the presence of Jim Keller at the Rudabaugh ranch, then of Levi's own decision to become a lawman. By the time Helen called them to supper, Levi was struggling with the necessity of revealing the purpose of his visit. He was spared by that supper call, but not for long.

There was little conversation during the meal. There was one place set that remained empty, but he did not think it appropriate to ask about it, and nobody appeared inclined to explain.

As soon as the meal was finished, Helen served coffee. Both of the women added milk and honey to their coffee, then poured the coffee into their saucers. They drank from the high-sided saucers, picking them up with both hands and sipping daintily. Both men simply drank it black from the cups.

"So what brings you here?" Westfal asked abruptly.

Just as abruptly, Levi answered, "The burnt wagon train." He felt both women stiffen, but Westfal betrayed no surprise.

"That so? How'd you come to be interested in that?"

"The father of one of the women that was supposed to be on it hired Pinkerton to find out what happened to her and her child."

"Do you think they were with that wagon train?"

"They were there."

Westfal obviously wanted to ask how he could be so sure, but he did not, and Levi offered no explanations. Instead, the rancher came to the point just as abruptly and bluntly as he had approached the reason for Levi's visit.

"And you figure I had something to do with it?"

The sudden anger in Victoria's eyes bothered Levi a lot more than he wanted to admit. Helen looked even more horrified at the idea than angry. Westfal appeared almost amused at Levi's discomfort.

Levi hesitated only briefly. "I don't know," he said. "Signs do point to that as a possibility. I ain't found out yet where they were headin'. It seems likely they may have been aimin' to homestead along the La Bonte. If they were, you'd have had a reason. It doesn't seem like something you'd do though. Not your style."

"You're right about two things: One, that ain't my style. Two, I don't want the crick homesteaded."

"I know you got your own hands on several places, so you can buy them out when they've proved up. I know you've bought out some others."

"You do your job pretty well. You're right. I buy out every one I can. I intend to buy all of 'em. It's my winter range. I won't give it up without a fight."

Levi sighed heavily. "I understand that. You can't kill people to keep it, though."

"I ain't killed nobody to keep it. Some of them homesteaders've been killed, but I didn't kill 'em. I hate that homestead law, and I hate Lincoln for signin' it, I guess, but I wouldn't have shot him either."

Levi thought about it for several heartbeats. "Do you have

any idea why those folks on the wagon train were killed, or who might've killed 'em?"

"Indians is what I heard, but I never believed it. That didn't make no sense."

Levi shook his head. "It wasn't Indians. There were arrows tossed around, but they were from at least four different tribes. Some were just old arrowheads someone had found, then tied to sticks. The horses were all shod."

It was Westfal's turn to think a while before answering. "I figured as much. I wanted to believe it was some band of renegade braves out to make a name with their tribe, but I was afraid it was going to turn out to be our own folks."

"They were most likely aimin' to homestead," Levi pressed.

"Maybe on the La Bonte." Westfal sighed again. He stared into his cup of coffee, then lifted it and drained the remainder of the hot black liquid. He wiped his mouth with the back of his hand. Finally he looked at Levi, and began speaking in a low voice. "Levi, we came out here in '50. There was just Ma and me, and a dream we had. We had us a pretty fair sized herd we'd picked up here and there, and three hands. We found this place, and thought we'd stumbled plumb into paradise.

"We built us a cabin, and some corrals, then a cowshed. It was lonely. The loneliness didn't bother me much, but Helen nigh went crazy with it afore we started gettin' neighbors. We started roundin' up whatever strays we could, and buildin' up our own herd. We did plumb good.

"It was hard. We both pertnear died with pneumonia one cold wet spring. I got snakebit twice, and nearly lost an arm once from it. I busted a leg and was laid up all winter, and

Helen had to run the place. The hands all run off once, and we was three months with no help at all.

"We had kids. Three boys, then Victoria here, besides two babies we lost. We lost both of them, just 'cause there wasn't no doctor close enough.

"We fought for every inch of this place. We fought blizzards every winter, and nearly froze to death tryin' to keep feed to the cattle so we wouldn't lose 'em all. We lost a-plenty anyway. We fought drouths in the summer, and short grass, and no water, except the crick that never did dry up, even in the driest years. We fought the wolves and the coyotes and the mountain lions, to try to save the calves. We went without food and without sleep and without friends and without all the things Helen grew up with, and she never once complained.

"Helen, she worked beside me and turned out more work than any two men on the place. Sometimes she was so tired and hurt so much at night that she even cried in her sleep, when she didn't know she was doin' it, but she never complained.

"We fought the Indians, sometimes. We made friends of some of 'em. We gave away some cows to 'em sometimes, when they was in a starvin' time, and they got away with stealin' some now and then. We hung a rustler from time to time, and some of them got away with our stock, too. But we made out good. We done real good. As a matter of fact, we got plumb rich.

"When the kids was old enough, Helen taught 'em. There weren't no schools, but she taught 'em better'n any school could've. I taught 'em my part. They learned to ride and rope and shoot with the best of 'em. Even my little Vicky, here – she won't let me call her that no more – she's all growed up and become Victoria now – but she's still Vicky to me – she can ride any horse on the place and outshoot most any man that comes along. We didn't teach 'em that to make 'em special. We taught 'em that so they could survive out here.

"We did our best by our kids. It wasn't enough, though. Our firstborn, William, died on his sixteenth birthday. He was chasin' two men that were stealin' cows from us. His horse went down and throwed him off and busted his neck.

"We found the two men and we hung 'em, but it didn't bring my boy back. Our youngest son, Martin, was killed just a year later, tryin to get a bunch of heifers in ahead of a big old thunderstorm. The lightning got him. Killed him and his horse both, right where they stood.

"We hurt more than I thought a soul could hurt and still go on, but we went on anyway. We stuck it out. We carved us a ranch out of this hard land that's just about as close to perfect as I know. But it's cost us more than I can ever tell you.

"Now these greenhorns want to come out here and lay claim to what we bought with our sweat and tears, and the lives of our own flesh and blood. They want to just walk up and take it, without so much as a 'by your leave.' They want to tear up the sod so they can plant stuff that won't grow here, and by the time they starve out or get killed, the land won't be worth anything to anyone no more.

"Well, they ain't gonna do it with my range! I've pretty much got it figured out how to stop 'em, and I will stop 'em. I'm getting' a grip on most of the land down the crick as far as my winter range runs, and I'll own it outright, sooner or later. It's my right. I built this place, and I ain't about to give it away. If they take it away from me, it'll be over my dead body.

"But I want you to understand one thing, Levi. I'll do it within the law. I'll do it within the things the Good Lord says is right and true. I'll not go against what He says in the Good Book.

"I might fudge the law, where I can, by puttin' my hired hands on places to prove up on 'em. They'll be hands I can trust not to bust the sod, and to live up to their agreement when they get a deed. That ain't the intent of the law, and I know it, and I don't care. I'll do it that way, and if it's against anything the Good Lord says, I'll have to ask forgiveness.

"If I have to, and I can't buy somebody out, I may try to scare 'em out. But I ain't a killer. I'm a God-fearin' Christian man. I ain't never killed a man in my life that wasn't tryin' to kill me, or tryin' to steal what belonged to me.

"I don't know what happened to that wagon train, or the folks that was on it. I know that whatever it was, I didn't have nothin' to do with it. And the sooner you can find out and bring whoever done it to justice, the better it'll be for me, and for the country as well. If you need any help doin' it, all you gotta do is let me know."

Levi sat in silence, digesting all the rancher had said. He wanted desperately to believe him. He also had a job to do. If Westfal wasn't behind the deaths of the occupants of that wagon train, who was? If it was Westfal, would he – Levi – be capable of confronting him? Arresting him? Killing him? If that turned out to be the case, he would have to do so with no hesitation. That was the trouble with the law. There was no latitude in its demands

CHAPTER 11

"Far enough, Hill."

The keeper strap was fastened on Levi's .45. He inched his hand toward it as he reined in his horse. "You're one up on me," Levi replied, keeping his voice casual. "I don't think I've met you."

As the young man spoke, two others had ridden out of the trees beside the road, and ranged on either side. Levi heard the soft scuff of horses' hooves in the road behind him as well, and knew he was hemmed in. There were at least five.

"I'm Richard Westfal."

Levi slowly looped the reins around the saddle horn. He reached up his left hand and pushed his hat back from his forehead with a studied casualness that belied the knot in his stomach. As he did, he gently touched his horse with his heels to turn the animal a little way, allowing him to bring the two men behind him into his field of vision.

"You'd be Butch's kid?"

"That I am, and proud of it."

"You've a right to be proud," Levi said, inconspicuously moving his horse a little more. He was now able to watch all five men without having to turn his head too much. "Your pa's a mighty good man."

There was a hard edge of bitterness in Richard's voice as he replied, "Too good to have the likes of you tryin' to cause him trouble."

Levi turned his head and deliberately stared down the two men who had been behind him. He noticed one carried his head to one side as if his neck were too sore to hold it straight. He recognized the group as the men Bodharma had faced at the stage station.

"I seem to remember seein' you fellows a few days ago. It seems to me you wanted to gang up on that dark-skinned man I was with. I'd have thought you'd have learned your lesson."

"You shot Schally," one of the men said.

Levi nodded. "Because he was about to shoot an unarmed man that'd just whipped the bunch of you fair and square. If I remember right, there wasn't a one of you that even managed to throw a punch."

The man's face turned livid, but he clenched his lips and held his tongue. It was young Westfal who spoke. "I didn't tell Pa about you shootin' Schally," he said. "If I did, Pa'd kill you. He stands behind his crew. He thinks Schally just left the country. But I got a score to settle with you. Right now, I just want to tell you to leave my pa alone. I'll only tell you once."

"Then what?" Levi asked softly.
It was Richard's turn to feel his face flush hotly. "Then they'll carry you back to Pinkerton in a pine box, the way they should've done when Doc first figured out who you were."

Levi's mind was churning. He was sure there was one more man, off the road, in the trees to the north. Probably Wade, he thought, with a rifle aimed right at his head. He was also sure it was not Richard's intention for him to ride away from here.

He shouldn't have stayed at the ranch the extra day. He told himself it was because it felt so good to have a bath, to sleep in a feather bed, to eat at a real table. He lied to himself. He knew it.

He stayed an extra day because he was so entranced by Victoria. Her dark eyes were pools he wanted to dive into and stay lost there forever. Her laugh was a finer music than she produced on the tall upright piano. She could talk with him about things few people in the country were conversant in. Levi had been extremely fortunate. The family that had taken him in and raised him were exceptional. Eleanor Rudabaugh was a very well educated woman, and insisted on an equal education for her children, even if she had to do the teaching herself. That had included Levi. As a result, he had been well schooled far beyond the McGuffey's Readers that had formed the beginnings of that education. It had extended to the classics of literature and poetry, the rudiments of both Latin and Greek, and a thorough knowledge of the Bible. He still carried, among his things, a New Testament in the Greek language, which he read regularly. Victoria was equally surprised that this rough cowboy could speak so intelligently in so many areas. Because he spoke in the familiar slang and atrocious grammar of the west, she had assumed he was not well schooled. She soon realized that was not the case. He had an incredible range of knowledge. He just chose not to flaunt it.

By the end of the first evening it was obvious they could not get enough of each other's company. That continued through the whole of the next day. The day following, Levi could not excuse his idleness any longer, and prepared to return to his investigation.

After Butch Westfal's uncharacteristically long speech of that first supper, nothing had been said about the burnt wagon train at all. Until or unless there were new developments, that issue did not stand between them. Levi was just the adopted son of Helen's oldest and dearest friend, and was treated as such as long as he remained.

He had left the yard a little before noon, heading back down the road that followed La Bonte Creek. He had ridden less than two miles when he was stopped. Now it appeared the extra day at the ranch might well cost him his life.

As Richard started to speak again, Levi suddenly dug his spurs into his horse's sides. He wheeled him sharply toward the brush at the near side of the road and yelled at the top of his voice, leaning down tightly onto the horse's neck. The horse responded with startling speed.

He spun from the road and lunged headlong into the brush. Levi heard the flat crack of a rifle, followed by a series of yells and shouts, then a couple pistol shots. Nothing came near enough to threaten his wellbeing.

Branches lashed him as they crashed through the trees and brush. Suddenly La Bonte Creek loomed directly in front of them.

He spurred the horse directly toward it, yelling into his ear as he did so. The horse bunched his hind legs under him at the edge of the bank and gave a mighty leap to cross the rushing waters. He landed in the shallows almost to the other bank. He lunged up the bank and into the brush.

As they entered the brush, Levi leaped from the saddle with his thirty-thirty in his hands. He levered a cartridge into the chamber and knelt in the cover. His pursuers broke into the clear at the edge of the creek, tightly bunched.

Levi jerked the carbine to his shoulder and fired three quick shots across the water. Hats flew from the heads of three, including Westfal. They wheeled their horses and plunged back into the brush, swearing loudly and profusely.

Levi returned to his horse and jumped into the saddle. Returning the carbine to its scabbard, he rode straight away from the creek, turning downstream only after he felt a safe distance away.

After he had ridden a mile with no further evidence of pursuit, he chuckled dryly. "They'll be a whole lot more careful next time," he said. "I wonder how they're gonna explain them holes in their hats. At least they know good and well I didn't want to kill any of 'em. They'll know I could've, too, just as easy. Might even make 'em think."

It made him think as well. He finally admitted what he was thinking. "If that hadn't been Butch's kid, I'd have killed 'im, instead of shooting his hat off. Now I've still got to deal with him. That was dumb!"

He rode a wide circle, then crossed La Bonte Creek again, then the main road. He rode where he had good visibility in all directions. He avoided being silhouetted against the skyline. He changed directions regularly, always angling toward the La Bonte Stage Station, following no predictable course. If he entered a clump of timber, he emerged anywhere other than in a straight line from where he entered. If somebody had spotted him, and was watching him, he offered no opportunity for them to get ahead of him and surprise him again.

It was nearly dark when he eased up behind the La Bonte Stage Station. He left his horse in the bottom of a draw and climbed to where he could see without being seen. He waited until a lamp was lit in the house Cordelia had pointed out as hers. Then he returned to his horse.

"Well, fella, let's wait till it's good and dark, then we'll slip up there and have a little talk with Cordelia."

For some reason he thought of Victoria Westfal again. Then he felt a twinge of guilt because he planned to stop to see Cordelia. He tried to reason the feelings out for a moment, then shrugged. "Better spend my time tryin' to figure out who waylaid that wagon train," he told himself.

An hour later he left the draw, leading his horse. He tied the animal loosely to a tree twenty yards from Cordelia's house and approached on foot. He tapped lightly on the back door.

"Who is it?"

"Levi Hill."

The door opened at once. "Levi! What a surprise! Come in."

He stepped in, moving quickly to the side away from the exposed square of light. The move was not lost on Cordelia.

"Somebody after you?"

Levi shuffled his feet, feeling unreasonably awkward. "Aw, you can't tell. As a matter of fact, I have been shot at several times lately, not to mention whipped real good once. I guess I'm gettin' a mite spooky."

"Well I would think so! You might even get the idea you're not very popular around here."

"You think not? Now I was almost sure they was all shootin' at me just so they could be the one to nurse me back to health again."

She giggled brightly. The sound lifted Levi's spirits immensely. "Have you had supper?"

"Well, now that you mention it, no. But don't go to any trouble."

"I was just fixing myself something to eat. Go ahead and wash up and I'll add a couple extra beans to it."

They talked about everything and nothing as she finished preparing the meal. After he washed, he sat at the table where they could visit easily. He was surprised at how right and natural it felt to sit there and talk, while she prepared their meal. It felt just as natural and just as right when she bowed her head and offered thanks before they began to eat. They were lingering over coffee when he brought up the matter he had come to ask about. Like the Westfal women, Cordelia had saucered her coffee, and was sipping it from the saucer. She watched Levi over the rim of the chinaware as he spoke.

"You said the ferryman at Bridger's Crossing might know something about the wagon train?"

Her eyes involuntarily darted to the windows before she answered. "It would be worth checking," she said. "I'm pretty sure that's where they crossed."
"I had heard that, but it doesn't make sense. If they crossed there, they must have been plannin' on headin' farther north and west."

"Not necessarily. We crossed at Bridger's when we came out here. We knew we were planning to homestead somewhere along the La Bonte, too. It was just the best place to cross with the wagons, and less danger of quicksand or bogs."

He digested the information. Then, abruptly, he changed the subject. "How well do you know Richard Westfal?"

Her eyes darted to the windows again, then back to Levi. She thought for a long while before she answered. "I think he's a very devoted child. He would do anything in the world for his parents."

"Would he kill for them?"

There was not the least hesitation in her answer. "In a heart-beat, if he thought he needed to."

"What about the men that ride with him?"

She hesitated a moment at that question, then answered. "Wade and Lonnie and George work for the ranch. For Butch, that is, but they're usually with Richard. Schally, Mick, Art and Jim don't work for anybody. I don't know if Richard pays them or not. I... heard some rumors that they didn't have any money at all, but not too long after the wagon train was burned, they had quite a lot of money all of a sudden. The gossip was that they had sold a bunch of stock at Cheyenne, but it was just gossip."

"Richard too?"

She shook her head. "No. He didn't do anything out of the ordinary. He never hangs around the station. He doesn't drink at all when he does come in. He never... He isn't involved with the women from the saloon at all. He really has never done anything, to my knowledge, that I would call wrong. In fact, he's probably the most careful man I have ever known to do nothing wrong. I don't know why I'm afraid of him."

Levi's eyebrows lifted. "You're afraid of him?"

She finished her coffee and sat the saucer down on the table. Her eyes were large as she looked at Levi. "When he looks at me, there's something in his eyes that scares me. It isn't that I think he would ever do something to me. I don't know what it is. It's as though his eyes don't belong to him. No, that's not right either. It's as though he is very, very near to being completely mad, but acts and sounds perfectly sane and normal. Does that make any sense?"

Levi finished his own coffee and sat the cup down. "Not a lot," he admitted. "Woman's intuition, I guess. I'll give it some thought though. Woman's intuition usually has some pretty solid basis. Richard and his boys waylaid me after I left the W-W."

She gasped. "They tried to kill you?"

"That seemed to be what they had in mind," he replied. "Either that or scare me outa the country."

Her eyes showed a depth of feeling that both thrilled and troubled him. She laid a hand on his arm. "Oh, Levi! Be careful!"

"I'm sorta learnin' I gotta do that all the time," he said. He rose and took his hat. "Cordelia, I'm much obliged for the supper and the conversation. Do you mind if I stop back sometime?"

Her eyes had that look again. "I'd like that. Any time, for as long as you like. But be careful. Please?"

He ducked out the door and stepped quickly to one side again. He burned inside at the obvious invitation implied in her words, and wondered if he were man enough to resist the desire to follow up on it. He shook his head and took a deep breath in an attempt to control his thought.

Against the darkness of the outer wall of Cordelia's house, he waited for his eyes to accustom to the darkness. Then he walked quietly to his horse.

"Don't shoot me, Levi."

The soft voice from the darkness froze Levi in his tracks. In spite of the request, his gun was in his hand."Who's there?"

"It's me, Wade."

"What are you slippin' around in the dark for?"

Wade ignored the question. "You saved my life when I got hung up. I owe you one. You gotta quit this country. Just ride out. You'll be killed if you don't."

"By who?"

"I can't tell you that! Just get gone. You're a decent sort. I like you. I don't wanta see you dead."

"You gonna shoot me if I don't leave?"

A third voice unexpectedly entered the conversation. The melodic accent of Bodharma said, "I think that is not his intention. He does not have a gun in his hand. If he tries to do so, I shall most neatly slit his throat while he makes the attempt."

Wade swore. "How'd you come up behind me? You just about made me do the most childish thing I've done in years. Just listen to what I said, Hill. I don't wanta see you dead."

A saddle squeaked, then hoofbeats pounded off toward the stage station. Levi sighed heavily and holstered his gun. "Thank you again, my friend," he said into the darkness. "I didn't know you were back."

"I have found what you sent me to discover," the dark man replied.

Levi shivered. "I was afraid you would."

CHAPTER 12

"You found 'em?"

"It is to be believed that I have done so, but one cannot be certain without some amount of digging."

"Where they at?"

"It is the ride of almost a day to the west and some to the south. It is near where the mountains begin. It is at the edge of a deep *wadi*."

Levi sighed. On a hunch, he had asked the strangely garbed one who had befriended him to look for a place a wagonload of bodies might have been disposed of in a hurry. He had hoped it would not be found. It had to be, of course, but now he would have to pursue its evidence to its ultimate conclusion. He shuddered at the thought.

"Do you wish that I show you where it is at this time, my friend?"

Levi shook his head. "Not yet, Bodharma. Let's ride the other way first. Do you carry a weapon?"

As if by magic, a long slender knife appeared in the man's hand. "There is this," he said. "It is not so broad a blade as your own, but somewhat longer. I believe it may also be sharper."

Levi's mouth curled up slightly at the corners. "You think it's sharper'n mine?"

Bodharma's smile spread across his face. In his other hand a red kerchief of silk suddenly appeared. Levi blinked. Bodharma's smile would have broadened, but it could not without enveloping both ears. He laughed aloud at Levi's expression. "Ah, I have so many surprises, my friend. Perhaps your own knife would be able to do this?"

As he spoke, he tossed the kerchief into the air. Spread flat, it began its floating descent. Bodharma held his knife, point upward, beneath the descending kerchief. As the featherlight fabric touched the blade, it parted, so the cloth slid down the blade with no discernible slowing.

Levi gasped aloud. "Let me see that cloth!" he said.
Still grinning, Bodharma carefully slid the cloth back off the blade of his knife, and handed it to Levi. Levi flipped it into the air as the other man had done, then drew his own knife and held it beneath it. When the cloth touched the tip of Levi's knife, it stopped. The cloth folded around the blade. It was not sharp enough to penetrate the cloth with only that cloth's own weight.

Levi looked back at Bodharma. His knife had disappeared. The man grinned at him with obvious delight.

"How'd you get it that sharp?" Levi asked.

"It is a very special steel. I do not believe one could find it in this country. Why do you ask about my weapons?"

"We may need 'em," Levi replied. "Do you carry a gun?"

"I have a rifle among my things. I am most dependably accurate when firing it. I do not carry the type of revolving pistol that you prefer."

Levi nodded. He thought for a long minute. Finally he nodded his head, agreeing with some yet unvoiced decision. "Let's ride," he said. "I got to have some more information. Listen. When we get where we're goin', there's a chance I might have to sorta pry some of that information out of a man or two. Do you think maybe you'd be able to scare 'em real good for me?"

"Why would I be able to frighten them? Why would you wish that I frighten them?"

Levi grinned. "You are a strange sight to folks that've never seen a man that wasn't wearin' either a hat or some feathers on his head. That turban, your dark skin, and the way you dress makes you look real mysterious to most folks. If you can combine that with the threat of something they don't understand, but it sounds plumb awful bad, they might just be tickled to death to talk, just to keep you away from 'em."

Understanding brought a rippling peal of laughter from Bodharma. "You wish me to appear to them as a jinnee?" It was Levi's turn to show confusion. As Bodharma pronounced the word, it sounded like "ja-nay." Levi said, "A Jinnee? What's a Jinnee?"

"It is a demon of legend among my peoples. It is a most very frightful demon that can appear as a human or as a monster of most frightening mien."

"Yeah, something like that, I guess. I want you to take a cue from me when I signal you, and just do whatever you can to scare the liver out of 'em, if they won't tell us what we need to know."

"I will do it! It will be most delightful, I think."

It was nearly sundown when they arrived at the ferry. The ferry was just landing with a one-horse buggy, driven by an older couple. They drove off the flat boat without a word. As Levi walked his horse onto the boat, Bodharma slipped aboard on foot, unseen. He positioned himself a ways behind the man, out of his line of vision.

"You Tug Riley?"

"That's me. Ride's two bits. Afore we shove off. Ain't no sense in it, though. You can pertnear walk your horse across. Of course, if you wanta give me your money and ride over, that's fine with me."

Levi fished for a quarter and handed it to him. "Are you the only one that runs this ferry?"

"Yup. And the only one for a good many miles up and down the river, as a matter of fact," the man replied. He spit a brown stream of tobacco juice into the river. "Like I say, you only really need it for wagons and buggies and such."

"Did you ferry the burnt wagon train across?"

The man's demeanor changed instantly. He had begun pulling the rope that propelled the craft across the river. Now he stopped, staring hard at Levi in the dim light of the evening. "I did, an' that's all I'm sayin'. They crossed here, they left here, and I didn't see any of 'em again."

"It seems to me nobody saw 'em after that," Levi replied quietly. "Did they meet anyone here?"

The ferryman's Adam's apple bobbed up and down. "I said I ain't sayin' no more. What makes you think they met someone? Why are you comin' around here tryin' to drag me in on what happened to them? Who are you anyway?"

Levi's eyes burned into the grimy old man. Even in the half-light, the hard glint in those eyes held him frozen. "My name's Levi Hill. I ride for Pinkerton. I'm here to find out what happened to those folks. I have ways to make you tell me everything you know, but I really don't want to turn a creature like that loose on a human being. You'd best tell me what you know."

The man's eyes darted around in the semi-darkness, then back to Levi. "What critter you talkin' about? You can't scare me. I don't know nothin', I tell ya."

"Then you have only yourself to blame. I didn't want to turn him loose on you."

Levi dramatically lifted his arms. In the deepest voice he could, he said, "I must know. Come to me." He pointed a finger, extended at arm's length, almost into the man's face. "This man must talk, or you must take him to the regions below."

Suddenly a tall figure, with his head swathed in a strange wrapping, appeared from nowhere. His clothing was like nothing the man had ever seen. The eyes of the apparition were long and sloped upward at the outer ends. Pointed teeth gleamed in the semi-darkness. A long knife flicked out, and a button disappeared from the front of the man's shirt.

The knife flicked out again, and a sleeve was split the full length of the arm.

The ferryman's eyes grew wide, until they appeared to protrude from his face. He turned so white he almost glowed in the growing darkness. The insides of his trouser legs became wet, but he didn't even notice.

Levi spoke again, in a quiet voice. "This is your last chance to tell me what you know. I sure don't want to turn this thing loose on you. It's so much worse than anything the Sioux or the Crow could even think about doing to you."

The man spoke, trying his best to make sense through his stammering. "Look! Don't let it get me. Please don't let that thing have me. I don't even know all that much. Honest. They just met someone that tried to talk 'em into goin' somewhere else to homestead, that's all. Then this here other fella, he shows up and offers to guide them to La Bonte Crick, where they wanted to go. They already knew that's where they was headin'. That's how come they crossed here. Only after they said they wasn't goin' to change their minds, the one that was bringin' 'em, he went and got hisself killed, so this other guy shows up and he says he can take 'em there, and..."

As he stammered, the man had been edging backward, toward the edge of his craft. At that point, he lunged over the side into the water. They could hear him, in the darkness, swimming wildly toward the shore.

Stifling their laughter, Levi and Bodharma took hold of the rope and propelled the ferry back to the side from which they had started. They retrieved Bodharma's horse, then rode downstream about half a mile, then crossed the river on horseback.

They arrived at McKee's trading post less than an hour later. They left Bodharma's horse a hundred yards from the place, intending to use the same ploy if necessary. Levi approached the ramshackle structure alone. He tied his horse to the hitching rail, and ducked inside the door of the building.

The lamps were lighted, lending a dim and smoky glow to the interior. Trading goods were stacked high, with narrow aisles to walk between the stacks. A table at the rear provided the only semblance of a counter.

Behind the table, Ike McKee sat with his feet propped up in front of him.

"Evenin'," Levi spoke first.

"What can I do for you?"

"Just lookin' for some information."

"I don't sell information. Just goods and ammunition."

"The folks from that burnt wagon train stop here for supplies?"

"Who wants to know?"

"Me. My name's Levi Hill. I work for Pinkerton. They stop here, did they?"

"They stopped here. That's common knowledge. They was headin' to La Bonte Crick, where they was all gonna homestead in one big long line. They had a fella with 'em they'd paid a chunk of money to take 'em there."

"What changed their mind?"

"I don't know that they did. Someone tried to talk 'em out of it, I heard, but they didn't talk. They wouldn't change their mind, even after their guide got hisself killed. Now that's all I know."

"Not quite, I guess," Levi said. His voice had dropped to that very soft and quiet tone. "I need to know who tried to talk 'em out of it. I also need to know who showed up at the ferry to guide them, after the guide got killed."

"Not from me you don't. If you don't want to buy somethin' you can leave now."

"No, I guess not. I guess you'll just plumb have to tell me what I need to know. Otherwise, I'll just have to turn a banshee loose on you."

The man chuckled. "Oh, it's a banshee is it. I ain't heard that word since my pa died. Plumb scared of 'em, he was. 'Course my ma, she had more sense. She taught me there ain't no such thing, so I ain't never been too scared o' seein' one."

Levi gave an exaggerated shrug. "Have it your way." He walked over toward one wall, with his hands held up, spread apart, above his head. With a twisted grin, the trader watched to see what sort of stunt Levi was going to try. Suddenly the figure of Bodharma loomed over him. He had neither seen nor heard him approach. He whirled around to look, when the big shadow was cast across him, and abruptly fell off his chair backward.

He scrambled to his feet and flattened against the wall of his trading post. He made no effort to reach for his gun. His arms were straight out from his shoulders, tight against the wall. His legs trembled so badly Levi thought he would collapse, but he did not.

Bodharma's knife flickered outward, appearing as if by magic in his hand. The trader's gunbelt dropped from his waist, the leather neatly severed with one effortless stroke. It hung there, upside down, dangling by the tie that secured the bottom of the holster to the leg.

Levi spoke again, in the same soft voice. "Like I said, I have to know who those two men were. Now I sure don't want to let this banshee cut out your soul and take it with him, 'cause I've heard the unspeakable things they do with the ones they're allowed to have. But if you don't tell me, I'll have to let him have your eternal soul."

The man tried to speak twice, but no sound emerged from his mouth. The third effort brought a squeaky-voiced, but intelligible answer. "It was young Westfal, from the W-W. The new guide was called Schally. That's all I know. The old guide, he got shot, right out here a-ways, just about sundown. I didn't see it happen. He's buried out back. That's all I know. I don't know who done it. Honest, I don't. Oh, Dear Gawd, don't let that thing have me!"

It appeared he was about to say something more. Sweat poured from his face. His trembling knees finally gave way. He either fainted before he fell, or as he landed.

Lips compressed to a thin line, Levi strode out the door. The tall shadow of Bodharma moved silently behind him.

CHAPTER 13

"I'm sorry to bother you this late again. We need a couple shovels."

Cordelia looked long and hard into Levi's eyes. She shuddered slightly at what she saw there. "You found them?" she asked softly.

Levi shook his head. "Not for sure. It seems likely, though. Bodharma thinks he's found the spot."

"What will you do if it's all of them?"

He sighed heavily. "Haul 'em back, I guess. Give 'em a Christian burial. Count 'em."

"Do you know who did it?"

He looked into the deep pools of her eyes, wanting more than anything, in that moment, to share everything he knew. He wanted to tell her how much he liked and respected Butch Westfal. He wanted to tell her how it would tear him to pieces if Butch was behind what happened to that wagon train. He wanted her to help him carry this impossible burden of damning knowledge. He wanted to ask her to tell him he was doing the right thing. He couldn't do any of that.

Cordelia pressed the issue. "Did you talk to the ferryman?"

Levi sighed, struggling with the conflict between the desire to confide in her, and the necessity of keeping things to himself until he had proof. "We talked to him and McKee, the trader, both."

He suddenly remembered the terror the sudden appearance of Bodharma had evoked in both the ferryman and the trader. He decided suddenly to trust Cordelia with at least part of the information. He sat down and thought a moment. The memory brought a smile to his face. Then he laughed.

"So tell me!" Cordelia pressed.

"You should have seen it," he said. "Bodharma slipped around while I was talking with them. Then when I gave the word, he just popped up, almost on top of 'em, looking as fearsome as any nightmare you ever had. They both thought he was some kind of devil, and that only I could keep him from stealing their soul. They were plumb willing to tell me everything they ever knew, and then some, if I'd just keep him away from 'em."

Cordelia giggled at the image his words called up, then sobered again at once. "Then you know who it was."

He drew strength from her eyes a long moment, then only nodded. Finally, he said, "We don't have any real proof yet. The next thing is to collect the bodies and get 'em buried proper. That's where we're heading now."

When they left, with two new shovels tied behind his saddle, it was fully dark. They rode with difficulty until the moon rose, then its soft light allowed them to travel nearly as fast as in daylight. They rode all night.

By the end of the night, Levi's stomach was tied in knots. That familiar cold wind blew down the back of his neck, making the hair stand out straight. Even his horse was nervous.

The serenity of the pre-dawn hours stood in marked contrast to the turmoil that churned within him. The wind had subsided to the merest whisper. The rich golden orb of the full moon was just setting over the jagged shadows that marked the mountains to the west. It seemed, in a moment's fantasy, to be scurrying away from the first rays of sunrise in the eastern sky, as though it didn't want to be around to witness what the sun would reveal that day.

Levi glanced at the tall figure of Bodharma. "You're too calm," he said. "I'm ready to jump out of my skin, and you look like you're riding to a picnic."

Bodharma's placid expression did not change. "It has been necessary, many times, that I draw from the inner peace of my soul," the dark man replied. "I have seen far too many things of great evil, in my long sojourn. Even worse, I think, than this thing we will see this day."

Levi mulled the thought a while before attempting to break free from it. "Well, at least you look better than you did at the ferry."

Bodharma grinned broadly at the memory. "A little charcoal can do so very much to make one appear frightening, can it not?" he agreed.

Levi grinned back, in spite of himself. "You did look fearsome, I'll agree to that. I never saw two grown men so scared, or so anxious to tell me everything they knew! I've heard of men scared enough to wet their pants, but I'd never seen it happen before."

Bodharma sobered at once. "It puts together the pieces of the puzzle on which you are working, does it not?"

Levi's dour mood returned. "It does for a fact, and I don't like what I'm learnin' one bit. I like Westfal! I sure don't want to think he's behind this thing."

Bodharma spoke softly. "But it must almost certainly be so. The man the trader spoke of is his son, is he not? The other worked for him. And is not this his land upon which we ride?"

Levi's voice was harsh and cold. "Yup. It's about as far south as he ranges, but it's his range."

"Does not that mean he is most surely the one who has done this, and then used this place, of which he already knew, to hide the dead?"

Levi considered the matter again. He asked himself all the questions he had already asked himself countless times. "I don't know," he said finally.

They rode in silence. Meadowlarks began their morning song. Their cheerful, lilting melody seemed out of place. Stubby Rudabaugh, the man who had raised Levi, had taught him to whistle that call when he was still grieving the loss of his parents. He had learned it well enough to get the meadowlarks to answer him, and it had provided him with much needed diversion. Stubby always said the birds were saying, "Oh-gee-whillikers," and it fit the cadence of their call.

Suddenly Levi gave the whistle, and was answered at once by a half dozen birds. Bodharma laughed aloud. "Ah, you talk with the birds too! You are an amazing man! Is that the way you solve the crimes that you are sent to investigate? Do you ask the birds?"

Levi smiled tightly. "You always thought it was a strange American saying, when someone said, 'A little bird told me.' didn't you?"

Bodharma laughed again. "If you could only do so in truth, perhaps we would not need to do this most unpleasant task before us this day."

Levi lapsed into silence again. They rode another thirty minutes before Bodharma reined to a stop. They sat on a high knob that commanded a view of a broad area of foothills. The land was cut at regular intervals by gullies washed by the downpours of summer thunderstorms. He pointed to the edge of a gully two hundred yards to their right.

Following the line indicated by Bodharma's extended finger, Levi saw it at once. The line marking the edge of a deep gully made a sudden veer away from it, then back again to the normal edge about a hundred feet farther along. The area within that half-circle was fresh dirt, void of vegetation, standing out like a naked scar on the earth.

"Dynamited the edge of the gulch," Levi said.

Bodharma nodded, saying nothing.

"Did you check it out?"

"I did not dig into it. I looked at the ground in the area around the place and saw there some tracks, including the tracks of a wagon. I did not wish to disturb the area without having brought you here.

Levi nodded. His lips were compressed into a thin line. He nudged his horse. "We'd just as well get to it," he said. Tying their horses to a clump of sage, they took the shovels they had gotten from Cordelia. They slid down the side of the gully. Levi stopped and looked up at the edge of the bank, towering a good fifteen feet above them. "Deep gulch," he said.

"It is deep, with a very high bank that was quite easily moved." Bodharma agreed.

With no more talk, the two men began to dig at the edge of the fresh pile of dirt. They dug steadily for several hours, pausing frequently to move large rocks aside. The sun was high in the sky when Levi's shovel struck something hard that did not sound like another rock. They both stopped, frozen in their tracks.

Levi straightened, arching the stiffness from his back. He sighed. Bodharma watched him, saying nothing. A deer fly buzzed past Levi's ear, sounding unnaturally loud. A trickle of sweat ran down his back. The cry of an eagle screamed faintly in the distance.

Two or three minutes of total silence passed. At last, Levi said, "I hit something."

Bodharma nodded. Levi lifted his shovel slowly, as though its weight had suddenly become intolerable. He pushed it back into the pile of fresh dirt. It bumped against the hidden object again, with a muffled metallic clang. "Two to one that's a wagon wheel."

Again, Bodharma only nodded. Suddenly both men began digging with a renewed haste, as though to lay bare the worst of their expectations as quickly as possible. It was swiftly apparent that Levi's guess was correct. The outline of a large wagon wheel soon emerged from the loose ground.

As they dug the earth away from the wheel, other dirt continually cascaded down from higher in the pile. As a large clump of dirt gave way and fell onto Levi's feet, a human hand was suddenly revealed. It jutted outward from the earthen heap, almost in his face.

He gasped, dropped his shovel, and leaped backward.

Bodharma straightened, looked at the hand, and softly said, "Aaah."

The stench of rotting flesh suddenly unearthed, filled the air. Levi felt his stomach lurch violently. He swallowed hard several times. He wiped his mouth with the back of his hand. He took off his hat and wiped his brow, then stood there, his weight on one foot, his hat hanging at his side, staring at the macabre discovery.

"It is exactly as we feared," Bodharma said.

Levi swallowed twice more. When he was finally able to speak, his voice sounded calm and steady. "We'd best throw some dirt back over 'em. That'll keep the varmints off. We'll go get a team. That way we can haul 'em to wherever there's a place to give 'em a decent burial."

"It is not possible to allow them to remain here?" Bodharma

asked. "Is the Christian manner of burial that only one can be buried in a place, or must proper words be spoken as each burial is made?"

Levi shook his head. "No, it's not that. It's just that we can't leave 'em here. The next big gully washer that comes along will wash most of the dirt off of 'em. Then the coyotes and bears and buzzards and magpies and everything else will eat on 'em, and scatter their bones to kingdom come."

Bodharma digested the information. Then he asked the question that was bothering Levi the most. "To whom will you go for assistance?"

Levi considered the matter for a long while. When he spoke, it was not to answer the question, but to ask another. "Can you keep out of sight?"

Bodharma's confusion was apparent. "I do not understand."

"I'll ride back to the W-W. It's the most obvious place to go for help, being closest and all. They'll send some hands and a team. But I'll need someone watchin' my back. If Butch is the one behind this, my life won't be worth a plugged nickel when he knows I've found 'em. If he ain't, then whoever it is will probably try to put a bullet in me. If you're keepin' an eye out, you might be able to spot anyone tryin' to sneak up on me."

Bodharma obviously did not like the plan. "If it is the ones you are riding with, who will seek to kill you, my presence in hiding will be of little help."

Levi nodded his agreement. "I don't think it'll be the ones sent to help that I'll have to worry about," he said. "If it is, I'll just have to take care of that myself."

His thinking had crystallized until he thought he had a pretty complete picture of what had happened, and who had done it. What he still didn't know was whether Richard Westfal was acting alone, or on his father's orders. He was certain he would know the instant he told Westfal of his discovery.

Either way, it was going to be the end of Butch Westfal. He suddenly wanted to be anywhere in the world except here, in this place, at this time.

The trouble was, he didn't have that choice.

CHAPTER 14

Levi caught himself with a start. He straightened in the saddle. He had been asleep again!

Another day had passed. Both he and Bodharma had been without sleep for three days. He could no longer stay awake and alert. Even his urgency would have to wait.

They rode back into the mountains until they found a spring, spilling ice-cold water from the base of a granite cliff. They hobbled their horses, cooked a meal, ate, and wrapped in their blankets.

The sun was well up in the sky the next morning, before either man awoke. While Bodharma caught the horses, Levi built a fire, made coffee and cooked their breakfast. When they had eaten and packed their gear, they rode out.

Levi rode alone into the W-W yard about mid-afternoon. Little activity was evident. Smoke curled upward from the cookhouse chimney and the chimney of the main house. The corrals were empty.

"Hello the house!" Levi called.

Two minutes passed before the door to the house opened. Butch Westfal stepped onto the porch, his gunbelt held loosely in his left hand. He didn't have time to speak before he was interrupted by another voice.

"Levi! How are you? Is everything okay? Get down and come in. I've been anxious to see you again."

Victoria's dancing eyes and bright smile made Levi wonder why he'd waited so long to return. He did not fail to notice that Westfal's expression was far less enthusiastic.

"Hi, Victoria," Levi smiled back at the stunningly beautiful girl. "I was hoping you'd miss me a little."

"Well, I didn't," she retorted. "I missed you a lot. Hurry up and finish whatever you and Papa have to talk about. I have a dozen things I want to talk about."

"Nothing deep or complicated," he responded. "I'm a little frayed around the edges."

Victoria's expression turned serious as she began to notice the lines of fatigue etched into his face. "You look it," she said. "Have you found something?"

Levi just nodded. Victoria looked like she intended to stay for the conversation, but Westfal murmured something quietly to her. She opened her mouth to respond, then shut it again. She turned and went wordlessly into the house. "Get down, Levi. Come in. Your horse looks like he's been rode hard and put up wet."

"So've I, to tell the truth," Levi answered as he dismounted. "I'm afraid I ain't got good news."

"I take it you found 'em?"

"I found 'em."

"All dead?"

"Yeah."

"How many?"

"I don't know yet. I started diggin' 'em out, to be sure that's what I'd found. As soon as I knew, I covered 'em up again. I need a team to pull the wagon."

"They're in a wagon?"

"Like I said, I'm guessin', 'cause I didn't dig 'em clear out. It looks like one of the wagons was used to load all the bodies onto. They drove it up against the side of a deep dry gulch, then dynamited the edge, so it buried everything."

Butch's voice was incredulous. "Just left 'em in the wagon?"

Levi nodded. He sighed heavily. "As soon as there's one big frog drowner, it'll wash all the dirt off of 'em. Then the varmints and such will drag 'em all over the country. All anyone would likely find after a month or two, would be scattered bones."

The muscles at the joint of Westfal's jaw bunched and worked. His eyes were hard as pieces of flint. "Didn't even give 'em a decent burial!" he said again.

Neither man said anything for a long while. It was Westfal who broke the silence then. "Where they at?"

"Nine or ten miles over south. It's about the deepest gully I've seen along there anywhere. It runs almost straight east.."

Westfal nodded. "I know the one. We call it Henry's Gulch, from an old trapper that used to run a line up above it. It's just south of a big old hogback that's got a lot of scrub cedars on it. You can see some spruce timber up higher to the west."

Levi nodded, confirming the location. "I don't know what to do with 'em, except to take a team, drag the wagon out of there, and just haul 'em all somewhere for burial."

"They're gonna be pretty ripe."

"They are that. Just one hand and arm was all I dug clear out, but the stink was about more than I could take."

Butch nodded. "Well, it'll probably be about like draggin' an old dead cow out somewhere to use for bear bait. After a while, you won't be able to smell it no more."

Levi nodded hopefully. "I'm gonna get awful sick if it doesn't work that way."

"You'll be wantin' to count 'em?"

Levi nodded again.

"Well, no sense runnin' off over there tonight. We'd just get there when it's too dark to work. Come on in. Spend the night. I'll have Charley get a team ready, and three or four hands. We'll ride out at first light. Go ahead and put your horse up and come on in."

As Levi mounted and turned toward the barn, Westfal

turned back into the house. Levi barely heard him mutter, as he went in the door, "Didn't even give 'em a decent burial. Left 'em piled in a wagon like a bunch o' coyotes!"

The evening was far more enjoyable than Levi had thought it could possibly be, under the circumstances. A bath, a shave and a square meal made a world of difference in his general outlook. Victoria's presence, and obvious delight in his company, would have made any time exquisite.

Butch Westfal remained morose and uncommunicative. He seemed lost in some distant musing, hardly aware of Levi's presence, and certainly unaware of the electricity that sparked between Levi and Victoria.

Helen Westfal was not at all oblivious to the fact, however. She noted the forming bond with approval. Her mind instantly leaped to something much more than just a good friendship. Nothing would please her more than binding her family to that of her dearest and oldest friend, Levi's foster mother. She busied herself with her embroidery after supper, and allowed the two to talk around her.

Levi and Victoria covered a wide range of topics, from the remaining repercussions of the Civil War to the classics of literature. Their discussion grew animated to the point of argument at times, but both enjoyed it beyond measure, and it showed.

It was with great reluctance that Levi went to bed. Long after he did, he lay wide-awake with the sight and sound and scent of Victoria in his mind. Every time he thought of her, though, the face of Cordelia was there as well. Her pert expression and saucy wit stood in sharp contrast to Victoria's soft voice and intellectual seriousness.

In the hour before dawn he was awake. He dressed quietly

and went downstairs. Westfal was already at the table, his hands wrapped around a steaming cup of coffee. As Levi sat down, Helen Westfal set a matching mug in front of him. He sipped it in silence.

Westfal's face was haggard. He had not shaved. He paid little attention to Levi. He drank his coffee and stared into its murky depths, as though there were something within it that only his eyes could see. When they had finished breakfast, he rose from the table.

His voice was brusque. "Just as well get to it."

With Levi a step behind him, he crossed the porch. His horse and Levi's were already saddled and waiting, tied to the rail at the porch steps. A team of Belgians were also harnessed and waiting. Four hands sat their horses silently. The first rays of sunrise streaked the sky as they rode from the yard.

They arrived at the site of the buried wagon by mid-morning. Nobody had spoken a word from the time they left the ranch yard. It was evident that Westfal had issued orders to his foreman, who had passed the word along to those picked for the gruesome task. None were looking forward to it, but none would shirk the duty. The weight of that duty pressed down upon them, however, and eliminated the usual light-hearted banter.

They attacked the pile of dirt with shovels, as though the turmoil of their emotions could be exhausted with physical effort. As the wagon came more and more into view, so did its grisly cargo. Bodies were piled on top of each other, in whatever position they had landed when they were thrown there. No effort whatever had been made to allow them any measure of dignity, even in death.

Anger smoldered in the eyes of the six men, as they worked. The stench of the rotting bodies was overwhelming at first. Three of the six got sick immediately. They retched their stomachs empty, then returned, white and shaken, to the task at hand. Nobody cracked any jokes. Nobody offered any encouragement. Each just wrapped a cloak of silence around himself and worked with dogged determination. After the first overwhelming waves of the heavy odor of death and decay, their olfactory organs fatigued. They could still smell it, but not as strongly. It became bearable. They were even able to step up onto the spokes of the wheels to clear off what dirt they could from the top of the bodies. When the macabre load of corpses was generally freed from its makeshift tomb, the horses were backed up to the tongue and hitched into place. Then the first words were spoken. They sounded loud and out of place after such a long silence.

"Who's gonna drive the thing?"

They all looked at each other as though they had just realized someone would have to climb up on top of it, sit down on that seat, and drive the team. Without a word, Butch Westfal climbed the front wheel and slid onto the driver's seat. He picked up the reins and slapped the team. "Heeanh!" he yelled at them.

The team leaned into the harness. Reluctantly at first, the wagon broke free from its prison of dirt and began to roll. Butch guided the team down the gully for nearly a mile before he found a place shallow enough for the team to pull the wagon up the side.

When the wagon rolled out on top, a strong westerly breeze struck them like a cold draught of spring water. It swept away the overpowering stench, and let them breathe air that didn't feel thick with death. As one, the five men on horseback and the one on the wagon took a long, deep breath, then let it out slowly.

Nobody rode on the downwind side of the wagon. It was nearly evening when they drove up to the plot of ground north and west of the buildings of the W-W. There were already a number of weathered markers in the little plot. Several fresh graves were already dug, and the rest of the W-W crew was busily digging more. The hands that had ridden after the wagon got shovels and joined them.

Westfal walked slowly to Levi. He looked crushed by some intolerable weight. "I couldn't think of no place to bury 'em," he said. "I decided they'd be as well off here as anywhere. I don't s'pose we're gonna be able to find anything that'll identify anyone."

Levi took another deep breath, grateful that Westfal had parked the wagon downwind from the cemetery plot. "No," he answered. "The best we can do is get a count, how many men, how many women, how many kids."

Westfal's head jerked up. "Kids? There was kids?"

Levi nodded mutely. Westfal muttered something, but Levi couldn't hear what he said. He didn't want to ask.

A stack of blankets was brought out. Bodies were placed, as carefully as possible, onto blankets, and wrapped individually. Levi took out a tally book and kept a record, guessing at the approximate age of each. Although they were afraid of lifting on any arms, lest they be rotted enough to pull off, the bodies were in surprisingly good condition. Perhaps the pressure of being packed so closely, or being buried in cold ground, had slowed the process of decay.

There was no indication that any had suffered any fate other than being shot, most of them more than once. None of the women's clothing was torn or missing. None of the men had been scalped or mutilated in any way. They had simply been efficiently and systematically killed, piled on a wagon, and hastily buried.

Three appeared to be teenagers. With great relief, they realized there were no children. They ended with a count of twenty-one men, nine women, and three teenagers.

"Thirty three," Levi said, as the last one was laid in the grave.

"Whatd'ya want done with the wagon, Butch?" one of the hands asked.

"Burn it. Pull it over on the rock outcropping, where it won't catch nothin' on fire. Soak it down good with coal oil. Even if we could get the stink out of it, I wouldn't never feel right about usin' it."

One of the hands climbed up on the wagon seat and drove it away. The rest of the men stood leaning on their shovels, waiting to be told what to do next. It was Westfal who spoke. "We got to say something, so we can get 'em covered up. Can any of you get it said without breakin' down?"

One older hand laid down his shovel and stepped a couple paces out in front of the two rows of graves. He took off his hat. The others, acting as one, did the same. The old cowboy said, "Lord, these folks come out here lookin' for land, most likely, and they got theirselves killed instead. Through no fault o' their own, we're reckonin'. We're askin' that you'd give 'em peace now. God rest their souls. And the ones that done this to 'em, well, we're askin' that you'd see that they burn in hell. Maybe it ain't right to, but I ask that in Jesus' name. Amen. Earth to earth, ashes to ashes, dust to dust. So let it be."

He replaced his hat. Butch's hand shook as he replaced his own. He turned to Levi. "Helen'll have a couple of tubs o' bath water on the porch, and they'll be gone off to the back of the house. We'll take off these duds and leave 'em for the boys to burn along with theirs. We'll never get the stink out of 'em. They're gonna just take 'em all an' pile 'em in the wagon when they touch it off."

As they trudged to the house, the thought passed through Levi's mind that the smell would never leave them, either. Whether anyone else could smell it or not, he would wear the stench of these deaths to his grave.

CHAPTER 15

"It's mine to do. I'll see to it. You just ride on out and tell Pinkerton it's been taken care of."

Levi faced the rancher he liked and respected so much. His heart went out to the man who had already experienced so much loss, so much pain. He wanted, more than anything he could think of in that moment, to simply walk away. He could not.

He met the flinty stare of Westfal squarely. "I can't do that, Butch. I have a job to do. I have to find him and arrest him. He's got to stand trial."

Westfal shook his head once. "I can't have that. I can't stand that. Neither could Helen. I'll deal with him. If it was my boy that did this, I'll take care of it. If he says it wasn't him, I'll know when he tells me, whether he's lyin' to me or not."

"I can't do that, Butch."

"He ain't a bad man, Levi. He's always been a good boy. The best! Even if he did do it, and I ain't sayin' I think he did, mind you, but even if he did do it, the only reason would be to protect me. He'd lay his life down for me in a minute. That boy well nigh worships me. Why, I had a horse that stacked me up, once. Nothin' special. He just spooked and started buckin'. Busted a couple o' my ribs. Why, I pertnear had to hogtie that boy to keep him from killin' that horse, just because it hurt me. And he was only twelve, then.

"He seen what it did to Helen and me to lose William. And then Martin was even worse. He knows what it would do to us to lose this place, our winter range, to sodbusters. If he did this thing, he only did it because he couldn't figure any other way to save Helen and me from somethin' we couldn't stand."

"That's not a reason to kill folks, especially women and kids."

"There weren't no kids! Even if he did it, there weren't no kids."

"There are kids somewhere. There were at least two on that wagon train."

"Then where are they?"

"I don't know. That's one of the things Richard has to tell me."

The rancher glared with stubborn belligerence. "You don't know it was Richard, I'm tellin' you! Aren't you listenin'? You don't know that at all. All you have on that is the word of two busted down old trappers, scratchin' out a livin' at a tradin' post and a ferry boat. And both of 'em spend most of their time sippin' homemade rotgut outa fruit jars. You can't go by what they said."

Levi sighed heavily. "There's more than that, Butch. There's a lot of evidence. I have to bring him in."

"Now you listen to me, Levi. If you go up against my son, if you try to arrest my son, you don't need to think you can come back to my place again. I don't care what your job is; you wouldn't be welcome here again. Ever."

They were interrupted by another voice. "Levi?"

Levi whirled at the sound of Victoria's voice. His breath caught in his throat at the sight of her. She had come outside without his notice, and stood in the soft light of the early morning sun. Her flawless beauty radiated in the soft light like a heavenly vision. Her eyes wrapped the warmth of their soft glow around him until he felt he could drown in their liquid depths, and gladly.

"Levi?" she asked again. "Levi, I know how hard it is for you, but I'm asking you, please don't go after Richard. Papa will take care of it. He'll do what's right. If Richard has done this, then it's because the fear of Papa being hurt again has driven him mad. People do go mad, Levi, and they're not responsible for what they do. There are things that can be done for that, though, and Papa will see that he gets help, and that he won't have a chance to hurt anyone else. That's if he is the one that did this."

"Victoria, it's my job to do," Levi said. His shoulders were rigid. His voice was low and even, but it rang with an iron resolve. "I've never turned my back on what I think is right. I've never gone back on my word. I've never violated a trust. When I took this job, I promised to do it fair and honest and just before God. I've never violated a vow I made to God. If I walk away from this without arresting Richard, I could never face myself again, and I could never face God."

A tear escaped Victoria's eye and slowly marked a streak of moisture down her cheek. She bit her lip. Then she took a big breath and faced him squarely. He could see the world-old promises in her eyes as she spoke.

"Levi, I—I know we've never really talked about it, and I'm being terribly presumptuous, but, well, I really care for you. An awfully lot. I—I hope you feel that way about me, too. But, Levi, I don't want your idea of duty to—to... Levi, I just don't think I could ever think of you the same again, if you cause the only brother I have left to be killed, or to spend the rest of his life in jail. Can't you just let Papa take care of it? Please? For me?"

A lump the size of a walnut swelled in the center of Levi's throat. The beauty of her face, the perfection of her body, the promise of her words, made his head whirl with a sudden and overwhelming desire. He had thought of her as a wonderful new friend, delightful to be with, but he had not allowed himself to fully consider her in this way before. The promise of her words swirled in his head. He swallowed hard. The walnut in his throat refused to budge. He felt as if a horse were sitting in the middle of his chest. He inhaled deeply, and let the breath out as slowly as he could.

Finally he looked fully into Victoria's imploring eyes. He sighed again. When he spoke, his voice was tense, but controlled. "Victoria, I have never known a woman as beautiful as you are. I've never enjoyed being with anyone the way I love being with you. The thought of spending my life with you is something I've never even dared to think about. But if I have to choose between you and God... if I have to walk away from my sworn duty... in order to have you, the price is just too high. I have to be faithful to God. I have to do the job I swore to do. I'll do it, or I'll die tryin'."

Victoria was sobbing as she spoke. "You can't just let Papa take care of it? Not even for me?"

There was no longer any hint of indecision in his voice as he answered. "It's nothing to do with you, or how much I want you, or how much I… love you. It's a matter of right and wrong. If I'd compromise right and wrong for any reason – even for you – then I wouldn't have any integrity left at all. The only difference between that, and someone who sold out for twenty dollars, would be the price. If my integrity was for sale at any price, then it would still be for sale. It's not. I'm sorry."

He turned from the pain of seeing the tears that coursed suddenly down her face. With his jaw set and his back rigid, he walked to his horse and mounted. He neither waved nor spoke as he rode from the yard. He had the sense of walking away from a chance he would never have again. It left him with a feeling of unutterable emptiness.

He was less than two miles from the ranch when his horse's ears shot forward. He was learning. The trouble with the law was that he always got the test first, then the lesson. But he had survived the test a time or two, and he had learned the lesson very well. He had learned his horse would sense another's presence more quickly than he could, and that second of warning could save his life.

The instant his horse's ears shot forward, Levi left the saddle in a long dive. He landed with a shoulder tucked under, and rolled, coming to his feet. As his feet touched the ground he stepped into the brush at the road's edge. His gun was in his hand as if of its own accord.

He stood without breathing, in order to listen better. The horse stood still, in the road, exactly where Levi had left his back. His ears were still forward, and he was looking intently at the brush just at the curve of the road.

A full minute passed. Neither Levi nor his horse moved. Finally a voice called out from somewhere in the brush. "Hill?"

Levi looked quickly around. If he answered, would it give his position away? Were guns even now trained on the brush, waiting his response as a signal to blaze away? Was there one man waiting for him or were there more? He edged silently backward toward the trunk of a large pine. When he had reached it, he answered, "Yeah?"

As soon as he answered, he ducked behind the cover of the large trunk. No shots replied to his voice. Instead, the hidden voice spoke again. "Hill, I'm lightin' out. I'm gonna quit the country."

"That you, Wade?"

There was a few seconds' hesitation. "Yeah. Yeah, it's me. Listen, there's somethin' you gotta know. The kids that was on that wagon train? I took 'em. I kept Richard from killin' 'em. I convinced him they was too young to tell anyone who did it, and we all kept our neckerchiefs up over our faces anyway, till it was all over. Except Schally, that is, and he's dead. Anyway, I took 'em up to Fort Fetterman an' left 'em with a family there. I just told 'em they was the only survivors of an Indian massacre. I know it ain't much, but I just wanted you to know we didn't kill the little kids."

Levi took a minute to digest the information before he answered. "So you're just going to ride away?"

There was a long interval of silence, before Wade answered. "There ain't a whole lot else I can do. I can't go back. God knows I would if I could."

"It ain't somethin' you can ride away from. Human life is sacred. You took it, for no reason. It'll be there, lookin' over your shoulder everywhere you go."

"Maybe. Time'll tell. Men have walked away from worse things."

"Not many."

There was no answer. It was Levi who spoke again. "How'd you set it up?"

Again there was a long silence before Wade answered. Levi began to wonder if the man had slipped away without his hearing him, but he doubted it. The answer finally came. "I guess you'd just as well know. Richard, he found out somehow that this Kit Blackwell was bringin' out a whole wagon train to homestead the La Bonte. Kit used to ride for Westfal. Richard, he just couldn't let 'em do that. They'd have tied up the whole crick for miles, and took most of Butch's winter range away from 'im. Some of us rode over to McKee's tradin' post to try to talk 'im out of it."

"I take it he didn't talk."

"He wouldn't talk at all. He was still sore at Butch. Something about him gettin' canned. He was gettin' paid good to show 'em a spot to homestead on good water, but he was mostly doin' it to get back at Butch. Anyhow, Richard saw he couldn't talk him out of it, so he called him out and shot him."

"It was Richard that shot him?"

"But it was a fair fight! He didn't back-shoot him or

nothin'."

Then he suddenly laughed, a short, hard laugh. "I guess I don't know how much difference that makes any more, huh? Anyway, then he sent Schally to just happen to drop by and offer to finish guidin' the wagon train to La Bonte Crick where they was supposed to homestead. But instead he led 'em roundabout to that draw, where we had it all set up to wipe 'em out."

"Whose idea was it to try to make it look like Indians?"

"That wasn't Richard's idea. That was Schally. He said it'd discourage others from tryin' the same thing if we just left 'em. The rest of the boys was afraid that'd point too straight a finger right at the W-W. Then he was just gonna leave all the bodies, there, and scalp 'em like a war party would've, but Richard wouldn't have none of that. He said we had a moral duty to kill 'em, but we at least had to bury 'em."

"You didn't do much of a job of it."

There was no answer. Finally, Levi said, "Where's Richard?"

Again the answer was a long time coming. "I figured you'd be ridin' after him."

"I ain't got much choice."

"I s'pose not. They know it too. They're waitin' for you."

"Where?"

"At the stage station. They got it figured out that you're sweet on that O'Connor woman. They're stayin' hid and keepin' watch for you to come around."

"And they just let you ride away?"
There was yet another long silence, before the answer came. "They don't know I've left yet. I 'spect Richard would feel he had to shut me up if he knew I was ridin' out."

"You know I have to arrest you, don't you?"

"I was hopin' you wouldn't. I was hopin' I could let you know where those kids were, and you'd give me a chance to ride away. It oughta be worth somethin' to you, to know about 'em."

"I am obliged to know about the kids. There's at least one of 'em that's got grandparents that will raise 'im and love 'im to pieces. He'll inherit more than you or I will ever see. I'm obliged to you for givin' him that chance. I don't know anything about the others. But I still can't let you just ride off. You helped massacre thirty-three people. You can't kill that many people in cold blood, then say, 'Whoops. Sorry.' and just ride away.

As he talked, Levi urgently surveyed his surroundings. As soon as he finished speaking, he moved silently back from the tree behind which he had taken cover. He moved swiftly back into the taller timber, where there was less brush. Then he circled toward the place from which Wade's voice had been coming. Wade continued speaking, but Levi's own movement, and the distance between them, prevented him from hearing the words.

By the time Wade had finished speaking, Levi had circled him, and was approaching him from the opposite direction. He spotted his horse first, and hoped the animal would not give away his presence.

"So what do you say, Hill? Is it a deal?"

Wade's voice was so close Levi almost jumped when he spoke. The man was in a clump of thick brush that edged the road, less than thirty feet from where he stood.

"Hill? You there?"

When Levi failed to answer, Wade swore. He backed out of the clump of brush. His gun was in his hand. He looked nervously back and forth toward the road, and toward the spot from which Levi had been speaking.

When he was clear of the brush, Levi spoke. "That's far enough, Wade. Drop the gun."

Instead of obeying, Wade whirled. His gun roared and bucked as he spun, but his shot was well wide of the mark. Levi's .45 answered twice in quick succession. Wade was driven backward by the force of the lead that slammed into him. He dropped his gun. He opened his mouth to try to speak, but no sound came out. He collapsed into a heap and lay motionless.

Levi watched his inert body for several seconds before holstering his own gun. Then he walked over, turned Wade's body over with his foot, and looked at him. Silently he shook his head. He wanted to offer a prayer, asking God's forgiveness, asking Wade's latest actions to represent an acceptable repentance, but he didn't know if the man had even been a Christian, before he had traveled so very, very far down the wrong trail. Silently he shook his head.
He retrieved the cowboy's horse. Lifting the body, he threw it across the saddle. He tied it into place with Wade's lariat. He knotted the reins around the saddle horn, took the horse to the road, pointed him in the direction of the W-W, and slapped him on the rump.

The nervous horse broke into a run, then slowed to a trot,

then stopped. He stood uncertainly in the road for almost a minute, then began to walk, slowly and steadily, in the direction of the ranch. Levi knew he would go home, carrying his grisly burden.

He returned to his own horse and mounted. He breathed, "Well, that's two. Schally and Wade. Five left to bring in."

CHAPTER 16

His feet made no sound. The moccasins which had replaced his riding boots allowed him to feel every twig on the ground. That sense of feel enabled him to step where no noise would betray him. He moved with infinite patience. He had spotted the lookout Richard Westfal had posted watching Cordelia's house. Then he had waited. The moon came up before it was fully dark, and that hampered his plans. Then a thick bank of clouds had moved across the sky, blanketing the moon, casting the earth into almost total darkness.

That was exactly what he needed. He approached the opposite side of the house from the lookout. The lookout was well placed. He could see both front and rear entrances from where he stood. His own outline was hidden by the large tree he stood beneath. There would be a short time when Levi would be exposed, moving from the hidden side of the house to either door. There was no avoiding that. He hoped the darkness would cover him in those moments.
He reached the side of the house without incident. He waited there until the lamp was extinguished, indicating Cordelia had gone to bed. He wanted no light inside, to be silhouetted against as he entered.

He waited for the clouds to be thick enough no light of the moon could break through. When such a moment arrived, he slid swiftly and silently along the wall of the house to the back door. He reached the door knob and opened the door slightly. He had not expected it to be locked. Looking around quickly again, he slipped into the kitchen, shutting the door quietly.

He stood there, listening for any sound, hearing nothing. He whispered, "Corrie? Can you hear me?"

He heard a soft gasp from an adjoining room, followed by the soft click of a pistol being cocked. "Who's there?" Cordelia's voice asked softly.

"Shhh!" he cautioned. "It's me, Levi. They got somebody watchin' the place."

This time her answer came in a softer voice than before. "Watching my place? Who? Why?"

"Richard Westfal and his bunch."

"Why are they watching my place?"

"Waitin' for me to show up."

"They're after you? Then you found out what happened."

Levi nodded, then realized she couldn't see him in the dark. He felt, rather than saw her move silently toward him. He felt the soft flannel of her long nightgown brush against him.

"Oh! There you are," she said, as she brushed against him. She moved to stand against him, so they could feel each other's presence. "You found out what happened?" she asked again.

He could smell the fresh clean scent of her hair. It caused sensations to arise in him that he could not allow. He had known he felt more strongly for her than he did for Victoria. He hadn't known how much more. He stifled the feelings that welled up within him, and whispered his reply. "We found 'em. Thirty three people, piled into one missin' wagon and buried in a dry gulch."

She gasped. "What did you do with them?"

"Got Westfal to help. Took a team and his hands and hauled 'em to his place. Buried 'em all in his cemetery plot at the W-W."

"Does he know Richard is the one?"

"He knows. He don't want to accept it, but he knows. He wants to find him and take care of him himself."

"He'd arrest his own son, and see him hang?"

"I doubt it. He'd probably kill 'im."

"He'd kill his own son?"

"I'd guess he would. It's what any cowboy would do for a favorite horse, that he'd had for twenty years, and had to be shot to put an end to his sufferin'. If it had to be done, a man would want to do it himself, as much as it'd hurt. He couldn't stand to have anyone else do it, and he sure couldn't ask anyone else to do it."

"But his own son?"

Levi interrupted her. "We got to get out of here."

"What? Why? I mean, I thought when you came in that you, that is, that I, I mean we... Why do we have to leave?"

"They're waitin' for me to come here, to get rid of me. When they find me there's gonna be shootin'. I don't want you here. Too much chance you'll get hurt. I want to get you away from here, then I'll ride back in at daylight, out in the open, when and where I can see."

"You're going to face them all? Alone?"

"It's my job. Besides, I got an ace up my sleeve. Anyway, I can't be riskin' your life."

"But there's four or five of them!"

"Five. Now go get dressed. I'll wait here."

She waited for several heartbeats. She laid a hand on his shoulder. Chills ran through him from her touch. Twice she started to say something, then thought better of it. Finally she moved silently away. He heard the rustle of cloth from her bedroom, as she pulled off the nightgown. Pictures immediately sprang into his mind. He forced them down, moving to watch out the window. It was almost total darkness. He could see nothing moving at all.

Five minutes later he smelled the fragrance of her skin again, then felt her brush against him. "I'm ready. Where are we going?"

"My horse is over in the draw. We'll go out the back door, slip along the side of the house, so the house is between us and the big pine over there. That's where their lookout is standin'. Then we'll go straight from the house to the draw. After we get to my horse, I'll take you over to the stage station. You'll be safe there."

"I'd rather stay with you."

Levi fought down that tide of feeling again. He hadn't expected the job to include this. He hadn't expected to find a woman he could respect, love, talk with, and one who was strong enough not to be offended at the necessities of a hard and rough life. He had never even thought of himself as attractive to women. But he had been instantly drawn to Cordelia. Then he had found Victoria, too. Now it was necessary to keep them both at arm's length, to fight his emotions as well as the external and potentially fatal battle. He knew she would never try to force him to choose between his integrity and her, as Victoria had done. Even so, there was no place for a woman in the life he had chosen.

He wished, suddenly, that there were no law to enforce, no crimes to investigate. Even as the thought flickered in his mind, he knew that would be even worse. God had equipped him with a unique combination of talents and strengths, tailor-made to be a man of the law. To have that unique set of talents and abilities, and no over-riding purpose for his life to utilize them, would be far worse, to him, than having to ride alone in the fulfillment of God's purpose for his life.

Maybe it would grow easier with time. "Let's go," he said. They moved as one through the door, shutting it softly. No sound broke the pitch-black stillness. No outcry came from the posted sentry. They slid along the side of the house, careful not to let their clothing rub the building, lest even that slight sound give away their presence.

When they had reached the hidden side of the house, they breathed a sigh of relief. Cordelia slid her hand into Levi's as they set out toward the draw. He held that hand to steady her as they walked in darkness, but he could not ignore the electricity that radiated through him at her touch.

At the edge of the draw they stopped, listening intently. After a few seconds, Levi heard his horse blow softly, and stamp a foot. Reassured by the animal's calm, he tugged gently on her hand, and they slid down the side of the draw. In the bottom of the shallow defile, he paused again. He could hear no sound out of place. They began to walk boldly now, side by side, toward his waiting horse.

When they were still a hundred feet from the waiting animal, the cloud bank moved from the face of the moon, bathing the earth in soft light. Because they had been straining so hard to see in the deeper darkness, it seemed suddenly almost as bright as day.

Cordelia moved over closer to Levi. "Oh, isn't it beautiful?" she asked, staring at the moon.

"We got out of sight just in time," Levi responded.

"You mean you got into sight just in time," a harsh voice corrected. "It helps to be able to see you."

Cordelia gasped. Levi released the hand he hadn't been aware he was still holding. He stepped away from her as he turned to face the voice.

Richard Westfal faced him. Two other men ranged to each side of him. Levi recognized them as the ones who had accosted Bodharma. All five had their guns trained squarely on him.

Levi's heart felt as though it stopped. He was trapped, without a chance. He had let his concern for Corrie get both her and himself in a deadly box.

"Let Corrie go," Levi said. "She's got no part in this."

Westfal laughed, one short, hard laugh. "Not a chance, Hill. She knows as much as you do. Sorry you gotta disappear, but Pa, he just couldn't take findin' out I'm the one that got rid of all them homesteaders."

He had to think of something, and quickly. These were men who had slaughtered a whole wagon train full of people, with no hesitation and no qualms. He wondered suddenly if they had served in the war. Perhaps its horrors had warped them so severely. Whatever the reasons, he knew they would hesitate no less in killing him and Cordelia. If he could keep Westfal talking, maybe he could think of something.

"Your pa already knows," Levi said.

Westfal shook his head. "No he don't. He thinks he does. You just about got him convinced. But, as soon as you disappear, I'll convince him it wasn't me at all. You see, he's been hurt too much. I just can't allow anything to hurt him any more."

His gun, pointed squarely at Levi's chest, never wavered. Neither did the other four guns, also pointed directly at him. He thought he could probably draw and shoot Westfal before he could react and squeeze his trigger. He knew his own phenomenal speed. He knew with deadly certainty he could not shoot five men before they shot him.

"He's a strong man," Levi argued. "He can handle anything that comes along, except maybe bein' lied to, by a son he's trusted."

Westfal shook his head emphatically. "No, he can't. I know

my pa. He's just about at the end of his rope. He's had too many crosses to bear. He's had his heart busted too many times. I made up my mind a long time ago that he wasn't never gonna have to face that kind of hurt again. I made up my mind that I was put here on this earth to protect him. I gotta keep the homesteaders away from his land. I gotta keep people like you away from him. I gotta take care of him. I'm all he's got left."

There simply wasn't any way out. He was going to have to try. Maybe he could knock Cordelia to the ground as he drew. That might provide some confusion and distraction, but it would also slow his draw.

Maybe he could will himself to keep shooting, even after they shot him, until they were all dead. That might save Cordelia's life, even though it would mean his own certain death. Then the despair of their situation struck him full force. There just wasn't any way out. He was going to die. Here. Tonight. So was Cordelia.

Levi's voice sounded tired as he responded. "It's the wrong way to do it," he said. "The thing your pa needs from you is for you to be honest and honorable. You need to be somebody he can be proud of, not somebody doin' unspeakable wrong to try to protect him."

Westfal's face went instantly livid. Whatever slender thread of sanity still held him, suddenly snapped. His eyes took on a wild, fanatical gleam. He raised the pistol he was holding and pointed it at Levi's face, shaking it like a scolding mother would shake a finger at a naughty child.

"Don't you go tellin' me what my pa needs! I know what he needs! I know! You don't. You don't know nothin'. You wasn't there, watchin' him, when he picked up William, and his head flopped over like it was just the skin keepin' it from fallin' plumb off. You wasn't there with him when he picked up Martin, and him smellin' like hellfire and brimstone, and all black where the lightnin' went through him. You didn't see the way he got old, just overnight, 'cause he couldn't bear the weight of losin' his second son in a year. You didn't see the way he stared off into nothin' for hours on end when he figured out folks was gonna start tryin' to homestead the crick. You didn't see none of it. You don't know nothin'. You just come here to try to destroy my pa, just like all the rest of 'em did, and you ain't gonna! You hear me? You ain't gonna. 'Cause I'm gonna..."

The mad tirade was interrupted abruptly. A hole suddenly appeared in the center of Richard's forehead. At the same instant, a single rifle shot reverberated off the sides of the draw.

The four men with Richard hesitated an instant, looking around in confusion for the source of the shot. It was all the advantage Levi needed. He didn't even think about what he was doing. He simply reacted to the instant's opening. His 45 appeared in his hand as if it had leaped there of its own will. It was thundering and spouting flame even as it came level. Three of the four men were already shot before the fourth realized he needed to respond. That final man squeezed his trigger, but the shot was diverted astray by two bullets that plowed into his body simultaneously. Neither was from Levi's gun. One was from a pistol that had appeared in Cordelia's hand. The other was from the rifle on the rim.

It was all over in a matter of little more than a second. The five men lay without moving. Levi turned to Cordelia. "You okay?"

"I'm fine. They didn't get off but one shot. Land sakes, Levi! I never even heard of anyone that could draw and shoot that fast."

"You did pretty well yourself," he said, smiling tightly. "The last one would've gotten me, except for you. Where did you have that gun?"

"In my hand," she said simply. "I had it in my hand the whole way. I just kept it against my dress, so it didn't show."

He shook his head in disbelief. "But I was holdin' your hand!"

She giggled. "I'm left-handed. You were holding my right hand with your left. You've never even noticed I'm left-handed."

Instead of answering, Levi turned and addressed the emptiness at the rim of the draw. "That you up there, Bodharma?"

The rich, musical laugh answered the question before the words did. "Ah, yes, my friend. You asked me to remain from sight and be prepared to assist you. I was beginning to believe my services were not necessary, until only just this moment."

"Your services saved my skin," Levi replied. "I hadn't even spotted you, but I was countin' on you to be there tomorrow. I'm sure glad you were there tonight. I'm not sure I could have shot Richard, even if I'd had the chance."

Cordelia looked at the five bodies. A shudder ran through her. "What do we do now?" she asked.

Levi sighed. He thumbed the empties from the cylinder of his Colt and replaced them with fresh cartridges from his belt. He holstered the weapon.

He sighed again. "We'll need a wagon. Someone will have to haul Richard and the others to the W-W. I'll tell my boss at Pinkerton where the kids are. I'm guessin' one of 'em is the grandson of the folks that hired Pinkerton to find out what happened. They'll be comin' out after him, like as not."

"I think the time has come for this wanderer to continue with his journey to California," Bodharma said. "It has been a most enlightening time I have spent with you, my very good friend. May you walk a long and happy road."

Levi extended a hand to the tall, dark man. "Bodharma, you're the strangest man I've ever met, and one of the best. You saved my life twice. I am much obliged. I won't forget you. I hope you find all you're looking for when you get to California."

Bodharma turned to Cordelia. "And you, ah, Madam, please forgive me, because I am yet finding it very difficult to talk with ladies, and more especially when their entire face is exposed. That is not done in my country, but I have been honored to know you. I have learned much from you too. I wish for you another opportunity to be married and to have many children."

Cordelia started to extend a hand to him, then thought better of it as she saw him start to recoil. Instead, she said merely, "Thank you. Good luck."

Without another word, the mysterious figure climbed quickly up the side of the draw and disappeared. Levi and Cordelia stood looking after him in silence. Levi finally broke the spell.

"Well, I'll walk you back to the house."

Neither spoke until they were at the door. There, they turned to face each other.

"What will happen to Butch and Helen? How can they stand to lose another son? Especially knowing what he did, and why he had to die."

Levi thought on it a long moment, before he answered. "It'll be up to you to tell them he lost his mind. He just went crazy tryin' to protect them. I don't know if it'll help any, but it might. You tell Butch, too, that I didn't kill his boy."

"What will you do now?" she asked.

"Oh, I'll go back to Cheyenne. I'll let that overstuffed chair polisher drive me crazy till he sends me out on another job. Maybe I can irritate him just a little more than he irritates me. Then I'll just go on trying to do my job."

"How long will you keep doing that?"

"As long as God keeps me alive, and as there keeps bein' them kind of jobs to do, I guess. And there will, so long as people keep wantin' what others got, or tryin' to kill the ones they don't like."

"That sounds like an awfully lonely life."

He looked into her eyes for a long moment before he answered. "That's the trouble with the law. It's a lonely business. It never really bothered me much, before I met you. But I guess some men were just meant to be lonely. It's what The Almighty made me fit to do."

"You could do almost anything, I think."

"Yeah. Maybe. But this is the job I can be happy doin', and

feel like I'm makin' my life count for somethin', and doin' what He wants me doin'." He laughed self-consciously. "Sounds pretty syrupy, don't it?"

She searched his eyes for a long time before she responded. Finally she said, "I think it sounds noble and high and beautiful. Well, I wish you Godspeed, Levi Hill. I'm glad there are men like you, even if I can't have you. I will never forget you."

She stretched up quickly and placed a soft kiss on his lips. Then she ducked into the house, closing the door behind her. Levi stood there, stunned, for several seconds. He thought he heard the soft sound of sobbing on the other side of the door. Then he turned and walked to his horse, mounting silently.

As he rode from the yard, his tongue reached out tentatively to savor the lingering taste of her kiss on his lips. It was a flavor he would remember during a lot of long and lonely nights.

The End

CPSIA information can be obtained at www.ICGtesting.com
Printed in the USA
LVOW131527030513

332228LV00001B/174/P